Kamezis, Panos.

Aberdeenshire
COUNCIL

Aberdeenshire Libraries
www.aberdeenshire.gov.uk/libraries
Renewals Hotline 01224 661511

1 1 SEP 2012

2 8 SEP 2012

ALSO BY PANOS KARNEZIS

Little Infamies
The Birthday Party

PANOS KARNEZIS

The Maze

VINTAGE BOOKS
London

Published by Vintage 2007

4 6 8 10 9 7 5 3

Copyright © Panos Karnezis 2004, 2007

Panos Karnezis has asserted his right under the Copyright, Designs
and Patents Act 1988 to be identified as the author of this work

This book is sold subject to the condition that it shall not,
by way of trade or otherwise, be lent, resold, hired out, or
otherwise circulated without the publisher's prior consent in any
form of binding or cover other than that in which it is published
and without a similar condition including this condition being
imposed on the subsequent purchaser

First published in Great Britain in 2004 by Jonathan Cape

First published by Vintage in 2005

This revised edition first published by Vintage in 2007

Random House, 20 Vauxhall Bridge Road,
London SW1V 2SA

www.vintage-books.co.uk

Addresses for companies within The Random House Group Limited
can be found at: www.randomhouse.co.uk/offices.htm

The Random House Group Limited Reg. No. 954009

A CIP catalogue record for this book
is available from the British Library

ISBN 9780099513292

The Random House Group Limited supports The Forest Stewardship
Council (FSC®), the leading international forest certification organisation.
Our books carrying the FSC label are printed on FSC® certified paper.
FSC is the only forest certification scheme endorsed by the leading
environmental organisations, including Greenpeace. Our
paper procurement policy can be found at
www.randomhouse.co.uk/environment

MIX
Paper from
responsible sources
FSC® C016897
FSC
www.fsc.org

Typeset by SX Composing DTP, Rayleigh, Essex
Printed and bound in Great Britain by Clays Ltd, St Ives PLC

In the shadow of a man who walks in the sun, there are
more enigmas than in all religions, past present and future

Giorgio de Chirico

Historical Note

In 1919, in the aftermath of World War I, a Greek expeditionary force landed in Ottoman Asia Minor with the apparent intent of protecting the local Greek population from the hostility of the Turkish majority. The true aim of the expedition, however, was the permanent annexation to Greece of the Mediterranean Ottoman regions, where a substantial Greek minority lived. The Greek occupation lasted until the summer of 1922, when the military tide turned in the Turks' favour. After a massive offensive that quickly turned into a rout, the Greek army was forced to retreat to the coast in disorder and evacuate Asia Minor.

The tolling of the bells sounded strange in the peace of the dawn. The sound travelled over the tiled roofs and across the abandoned town, where dismantled artillery guns lay among iron bedsteads, oak tables and broken wardrobes. Leaning against a wall was an old postman's motorcycle. Shreds of velvet curtains were flapping at one of the windows of a big house. A cloud of red dust entered the living room, carrying earth from the plain, shrivelled rosebuds and pieces of parched paper. In the once majestic room only remained a gutted crimson sofa, the fringed corner of a carpet, a chessboard table whose top had been scraped by a knife. On the wooden parquet, next to a heap of compost and dried flowers, lay a leopard skin with no head, tail or paws. At the other end of the room, what seemed like the prow of a small boat was in fact the front of a big bath in whose hull someone had expressed his contempt by an irreverent act of defecation.

A sudden dash over the floorboards broke the silence: a rat making its way across the devastation, stopped briefly to sniff the air. It crossed the shafts of sunlight, passed through a crack in the French windows and came out to the veranda. In the gardens a careful stomping had crushed the beds of flowers and herbs. A cherry tree had been attacked with an axe, and its leaves had since dried and fallen off. When the sun came out, a bevy of crows on its branches took flight.

Uprooted shrubs tumbled down the dirt streets. Past an open conduit filled with dried excrement lay a maze of narrow alleyways – no one was to be found in those poorer houses either. In the square the Town Hall had been set on fire, and its roof had caved in. The crows flapped towards the outskirts of the town. Some distance beyond the last houses, in the middle of the country road, lay the carcasses of dead water buffalo still yoked to wagons loaded with loot that was covered in dust: pieces of furniture, a silent grandfather clock, a heavy Victrola. The crows landed on the dead animals, which were in a stage of advanced putrefaction: the exodus must have taken place several weeks earlier.

The sun climbed higher. The wind turned the wheels of the abandoned carriages. A pair of crows fought over a piece of rotten meat. The tolling of the church bells stopped. A spring day was beginning. Slowly, the plain erased the town from the eternal Anatolian landscape.

Part 1

The Retreat

1

Brigadier Nestor sat up in his cot and rubbed his eyes, which were faint and colourless as if his eternal habit of rubbing them with his knuckles had worn their sheen. He yawned and unlocked the trunk with a set of keys that hung from his neck. The trunk was packed with pressed and neatly folded clothes some of which he had not yet worn on this tour of duty: a parade uniform with medals and ribbons, another black uniform for evening functions with satin lapels and gold epaulettes, a short riding tunic with coloured lanyards. He rummaged through the trunk. Under a pair of patent-leather boots with silver spurs he found the bundle with his correspondence, everything his wife had sent him since the beginning of the war: Christmas and Easter cards, newspaper clippings, a postcard of a spa by the sea, a child's crayon drawing. He pulled off the rubber band that held the letters together and let them drop to the floor.

It was hot and dark in the back of the lorry. A canvas stretched over the roof and the sides, letting no light in or heat out. Brigadier Nestor felt nauseous. His throat was dry, but he craved neither a drink nor fresh air. He stood up and struggled to keep his balance while the moving lorry rocked from side to side. He stepped over his correspondence, leaned over the stove, lifted the lid of the pot with a pair of tongs and removed the glass hypodermic syringe. He drew from a little vial, rolled up his sleeve, fastened the rubber band tight above his elbow and injected the morphia.

5

The lorry continued its journey in and out of the potholes. Blasts of hot dust fell on the tarpaulin like pot shots. The exhaust backfired, and the smell of petrol brought Brigadier Nestor round like an unwelcome sniff of smelling salts. The sun cast the shadow of the vehicle on the saltpetre: a big scarab crawling slowly in the heat. There were barren hills all round. The side of the track was scattered with the bleached bones of birds and camels. Feeling the morphia in his blood, the brigadier rolled his eyes and smiled. Soon the drug had erased both his tiredness and his thirst. The suspension creaked, and a tin cup rolled across the floor. The wind carried over the padre's voice.

'. . . *When the poor and the needy seek water and there is none, and their tongue faileth for thirst, I the Lord will hear them, I the God of Israel will not forsake them.*'

For a moment the brigadier forgot the horror and felt adrift in a tranquil sea. The sea was their destination – albeit not the ultimate one; that was the motherland. But if they reached the coast, they would have a good chance of salvation. His eyes watered from the petrol fumes. Only now did he register the explosions of the battered exhaust, but his intoxicated reason misinterpreted them. Were they being fired at? But he felt little alarm, as if an ambush were not a threat but a mere inconvenience. While the lorry was driving round a bend, a little light came through the crack of the hatch, and the dust in the carriage sparkled. Outside, the vultures circled the walking soldiers and croaked impatiently.

'*I will open rivers in high places, and fountains in the midst of the valleys. I will make the wilderness a pool of water, and the dry land springs of water.*'

The brigade had been on the move since dawn. What time was it? Brigadier Nestor only knew it was daytime, it was hot, and they were still in the wilderness. How long ago had they entered this maze? Had he been sober he could have answered, but the morphia had swallowed up his memory.

On the horizon whirlwinds of dust shot upwards. The old officer coughed. His eyes grew heavy, and he dropped back on his cot.

'*I will plant in the wilderness the cedar, the shittah tree, and the myrtle, and the oil tree; I will set in the desert the fir tree, and the pine, and the box tree together.*'

The reciting voice drifted away, and the brigadier sank into a dreamless sleep.

In August the waiting had been over. That morning the sun had risen red and ominous. Under the sun the line of the horizon had appeared like a line made of sympathetic ink, and soon the rest of the Anatolian steppe was revealed, an endless plateau interrupted by a few hills, shrubs of myrtle and ancient ruins. Then it began. The artillery barrage had signalled the beginning of the enemy offensive. The guns had pounded the trenches, and then, as soon as the batteries had ceased fire, the infantry had emerged from the pall of smoke. There were ten divisions at the front, and the enemy came in waves behind its bayonets, panting. They ran across the barren plain, up the fortified hills, and neither the barbed wire nor the machine guns could stop them. The dead piled up in the gullies, but more men came until one after another every stronghold was overwhelmed.

Brigadier Nestor had been in bed when the offensive had begun. The evening before he had attended a dance at a nearby town that had continued into the night. He had welcomed the invitation, presented to him by the president of the local social club because the long uneventfulness on the front had numbed his senses. He had strong views about the situation and had made these known to his superiors: the present inactivity was not prolonging peace but increasing the likelihood of a disaster. But for some time his frustration, like that of many officers and soldiers, had given way to apathy. At the dance, when he was ambushed by a cheerful group of ladies and merchants, he had refused to discuss the status quo, saying only that in his opinion the front line was the sharp edge of a knife stuck into the enemy's side, and those who believed that there could be peace without it being carefully extracted were deluding themselves. That evening he had stood most of time at the buffet, tasting the food, and only after midnight, when the brass band had played *Rosen aus dem Süden*, had he allowed himself to yield to the pleas of a luminous beauty and made the brave, for a man of his age, decision to dance in the Viennese style. The waltz was still ringing in his ears when the enemy bombardment had begun at dawn.

It was all over in two days. On the landscape soon lay decomposing bodies, abandoned garrisons and telegraph poles with cut wires. What remained of the army, split into lawless units that ignored orders and fled for their lives: the war in Asia Minor had been lost. In the whirlpool of the defeat, Brigadier Nestor's decimated unit, less than a thousand men, had preserved its discipline and was trying to find a way out of the maze and reach the sea. They had to avoid contact with the enemy. They had been travelling for days, changing direction every time they suspected an ambush ahead, but there had been no sight of the coast as yet. Furthermore, communication with General Headquarters had been lost, and many suspected that the rest of the Expeditionary Corps had by now evacuated the peninsula.

In any case, Brigadier Nestor refused to raise the white flag.

The first thing he did when he awoke was to hide the syringe under his cot. It was late afternoon, and the column had halted. There was the snorting of horses outside, and the occasional clop of a shod hoof on stone. Brigadier Nestor sat back and crossed his hands over his belly. He felt contented even though he knew that his emotions were only due to the morphia; he had grown to accept its effect without shame.

After a while he sat up and tried to open a cigar box with a bayonet. He was still struggling when a younger officer climbed into the lorry and gave a casual salute. His uniform was caked with dust, his kepi was missing its cockade and a towel was tucked into its back to cover the nape of his neck. Brigadier Nestor looked fleetingly at his subordinate. His eyes narrowed in disapproval.

'It's you, Porfirio,' he said. 'I mistook you for Don Quixote.'

His Chief of Staff wiped his face on his cuff. He did not reply; he was used to comments like these. Through the open hatch, the dust of the plain blew in, settling on the blankets, the maps, the smoking coffee pot on the stove. With his face clean, the major looked much younger.

'Is it time?' the brigadier asked.

The radiotelegraph was in a corner, next to the old bicycle that drove its magneto. Without replying, Major Porfirio sat on the seat. Kept an inch above the floor, the rear wheel was set in motion with a hissing sound. The major pedalled with a sense of duty. There was a certain desperation in the task that seemed like a game, carried out among the dusty utensils, the small stove, the table with the yellowed maps.

For the next hour, Brigadier Nestor sent messages and waited for a reply but heard only electromagnetic noise. Finally, he gave up with a shrug of his shoulders. His Chief of Staff wiped his forehead and stopped pedalling. They had failed again. For the past week they had been trying to contact General Headquarters, but the only replies they received were a message from the enemy calling on them to surrender and a prayer keyed by the operator of the wireless on board a Greek cargo ship nearing Suez. The brigadier sighed and poured two coffees. As soon as he took a sip, he grimaced.

'Coffee without sugar should have been the punishment of Sisyphus,' he said.

9

He had awakened that morning to discover that the tin with the sugar had disappeared. At first he had suspected his orderly, but several witnesses had confirmed that the boy had spent the night in the infirmary, recovering from snakebite. There were no other suspects. Brigadier Nestor threw his hands in the air.

'A breakdown of discipline. If only I knew who stole it.'

He set his cup on the floor and took the cigar box again. On its lid, an African with a fez had smoke coming out of his ears. The brigadier tried to break the seal again with the bayonet. It slipped, and he cut his finger. The box hit the floor. The old officer set to sucking his finger. At his feet the caricature of the African mocked him. The major lifted up the box, took a switchblade from his pocket and worked its tip into the groove of the seal. When at last he heard the metal break, the brigadier let out a sigh of relief and welcomed the scent of tobacco. For a while the two men smoked.

'I miss reading the papers,' said the brigadier.

'There'd be nothing to read. When the situation took a turn for the worse, they started printing the old stories with the names and dates changed.'

Brigadier Nestor agreed that the censorship had affected the quality of the news, but any newspaper would be better than none at all. He shoved his hand under his cot and pulled out a large book. The spine read *Lexicon of Greek and Roman Myths* in fading letters. In its creased pages, several lines were underlined by a shaky hand. He tapped the cover with his finger.

'A most pleasurable read. The padre is incensed that I know more of this by heart than the Bible.'

The major glanced at the book. Behind the desk the rusty bicycle stood like a relic of old, carefree times. Pleasure felt to the officer more like an old fable than a memory. He put out his cigar, hid it in his pocket and spread a map over his knees.

'Well,' he said. 'We're lost.'

'But there is always the possibility of divine intervention,' his commanding officer said wryly.

The major leaned over the map.

'Our last confirmed position is three days old,' he said. 'But the track we're on now is not on the map.'

'Maybe it's the road to perdition,' the brigadier said.

A bird's cry came from afar, sounding like a curse. Feeling queasy from the heat, Major Porfirio took a sip of coffee, but it did not help. He put down his cup.

'I didn't like this campaign from the start,' he said. 'We don't know the first thing about this terrain.'

'What's there to know? East, west, north, south. It's not a visit to the attractions.'

'If it were that simple, we'd be home by now.'

Brigadier Nestor turned serious.

'Discipline is needed now more than ever, major.'

Major Porifiro let his eyes wander from the pot on the stove to the envelopes strewn across the floor, to the belt with the revolver that hung from the roof of the lorry: a world summed up in a few disparate items. It was like life in a prison cell: nothing else mattered. Brigadier Nestor sneezed.

'Damn this dust. It's giving me an allergy.' He sniffed. 'Naturally, I understand your disappointment under the circumstances. But rest assured, this story isn't over. Now we are down – but.'

The major went back to studying the map.

'Not to mention our Christian brothers here in Anatolia,' continued his superior. 'They shall need our help again.'

The morphia was making him eloquent. He looked to the past; it seemed to be a few inches above the major's head.

'Once there was an empire, major.'

The younger officer arched his eyebrows.

'An empire?'

11

'The Byzantine Empire.'

'A long time ago, brigadier.'

'History is what happens over centuries, not yesterday,' Brigadier Nestor said.

He sipped his coffee and drew on his cigar, savouring the mentholated smoke. The sun was setting, and he asked for his greatcoat. Through the open hatch, he watched a scudding cloud with a lone castaway's expression. It travelled over the plain, over the hills, over the sea, casting no shadow. He handed over his cup and cracked the joints of his fingers. The drug had afforded him its brief windfall and was now receding. If only he could sustain the feeling a little longer . . . Brigadier Nestor tried to remember the time he did not need chemistry. His subordinate poured the remains of both cups back in the pot and asked, 'Any orders?'

The effect of the morphia was evaporating. Brigadier Nestor wrapped himself in his coat and waved the major away. 'No. Dismiss.' When Major Porfirio turned to leave, the old man spoke again: 'Only—' He gave his subordinate a tender look. There was a hint of honest concern in what he said next:

'—not to forget what I said about discipline, Porfirio. I know I can trust *you*. But the brigade isn't just people like you and me. Make sure they all understand that in times like this the firing squad works overtime.'

The major nodded.

'Anything else?'

'Go.'

The old officer waited until the footsteps had faded away. He buttoned up the flaps of the tarpaulin and found the syringe he had hidden under his cot. A whistle blew outside, and the order to start again travelled down the column. For a quiet moment, Brigadier Nestor held the syringe to the light and smiled at it with disaffection.

*

'A little more?' Father Simeon asked, holding out his mess tin with both hands. His left eye looked straight at the cook, but the other was trained somewhere to the right and above the man's head. That eye was made of glass: Father Simeon had been wounded during a barrage of artillery fire in the first year of the expedition. Despite the warnings of the soldiers, he had rushed to give the last rites to a cavalryman lying in the field. A piece of shrapnel had hit the ground near him, penetrated the belly of the man's dead horse and caught the padre in the face. For several days afterwards, Father Simeon had worn an eye-patch until the brigade had taken over the next town. There the padre had bought a glass eye from a local taxidermist.

Father Simeon held out the tin.

'The day of Saint Euphrosynos is coming up, friend. Eleventh of September.'

The cook looked at him.

'Patron saint of cooks,' the padre said. 'I'll put in a good word for you.'

He was in his fifties. Despite the eye wound and the clerical beard, his face was still handsome and lively. For many years he had been the pastor of a small congregation in a village that offered few opportunities for sin. Boredom was one of the two reasons he had volunteered for the campaign; the other was his sense of not having fulfilled the requirements of his vocation. As a young priest, he had toyed with the idea of joining the Orthodox Mission in Africa, but in the pages of an illustrated novel he had come across an explorer swimming in a boiling cauldron and natives dancing all round him. The drawing had stuck in his mind, and he had quickly forgotten his divine calling. His decision had left him with an eternal sense of guilt.

The cook puffed with impatience: 'No more.' He shooed away the flies with his ladle. 'The mechanic needs it for the lorries.'

The padre refused to go away.

'Don't betray the souls of your comrades for some pistons,' he said.

A buzzard landed at the rubbish heap and walked around it, keeping an eye on the two men. Other birds plunged from the sky into the rotting matter. The earth felt hard and dry. Father Simeon counted the months that had passed since it had last rained. Trying to imagine the life of the old Christian hermits, a sense of worthlessness came over him. The cook began to clean the stove.

'How about that oil, friend?' the padre asked.

'It's against orders.'

'Don't worry about secular power. One should comply with the wishes of the Divine. When we get home I'll personally ask the bishop to reward you for your piety.'

The cook opened the oven door and put his head inside.

'Not even your patron saints can save us.'

Father Simeon's eyes fell on the cook's back: the man's trousers were ripped at the seam. The padre walked round to the other side of the stove to avoid the spectacle.

'Very well,' he said. 'Five.'

The cook took his head out of the oven and grinned.

'Ten.'

'I only have seven, sinner.'

The cook agreed. He wiped his hands on his apron, picked up the burnt pan and filled the padre's tin to the brim. Father Simeon looked around. On the rubbish heap, the birds flapped their wings and buried their beaks in the trash. There were no soldiers in sight. He unbuttoned his tunic, took out a package and handed it to the cook in return for the oil. The man passed it under his nose and sniffed.

'Not bad,' he said.

The padre contemplated the packet with sadness.

'I may burn in Hell,' he said. 'But life is a matter of priorities.'

He walked away with the mess tin in his hands. The air was

cool, but the earth was still hot. On the other side of the camp was a shabby tent, patched up with old uniforms and tablecloths. Above its entrance was an inscription that read: HOLY ORTHODOX CHURCH OF THE CAPPADOCIAN FATHERS. Once inside, the padre poured the contents of his tin through a tea strainer, funnelled the clean oil into an earthen pot and topped up the lamp in front of the altarpiece. Then he sat on the floor, made himself a cup of tea and drank slowly.

The poverty of the makeshift temple somehow added to its holiness. Almost everything had been put together by the padre's hand: the broken lectern fixed on a machine-gun tripod, the cases of artillery shells filled with dirt and used as candelabra, the doors hinged together to make an altarpiece. In the middle of the tent was a brazier filled with charcoal. He kindled it with a bundle of handbills daubed with spirit. While waiting for the fire to build, he glanced at the little pieces of paper he had found that morning pinned on the entrance to his tent. Handbills advocating insurgency had been appearing throughout the campaign under trunks, knapsacks and saddles. The first had been distributed the very day of the landing. As soon as the troopship with the first detachment of the brigade had dropped anchor, its decks had been swarmed with the paper squares the soldiers would soon grow familiar with. Blown by the wind, they had reached the promenade, where a crowd had assembled to welcome the liberators. It had been an embarrassing incident that had almost cost Brigadier Nestor his command. Since then a number of inquiries had been undertaken, but none had revealed the culprit. Father Simeon had preached against the handbills on several occasions, but they continued to appear.

It was time. He took out his cross from his pocket and wore it over his uniform, then put his stole about his shoulders. He dressed with slow movements, whistling and taking his time to pluck the loose threads of his stole. Having lived alone all his life, he had invested his domestic and religious chores with

15

a transcendental quality. A set of vestments, a bed made, a steaming pot: specks of life were everywhere. When he was ready, he stepped out of the tent and shook his handbell. No one came. He rang the bell louder. As soon as he stopped, silence returned to the camp. He tried a third time. A dog squirmed out from underneath a lorry and came towards him, its ribcage swinging to and fro. Breathing thirstily, it raised its head and looked at Father Simeon with dull eyes. Once the padre was convinced that no one was coming to mass, he removed and folded his stole, dropped his cross in his pocket and put on his skullcap.

'They've offered themselves to the Devil, Caleb.'

A month earlier more than forty soldiers used to come to the evening service, but by last week the number had dropped to ten. The evening before he had said mass to one deaf bombardier. Father Simeon snapped his fingers, and the dog sprang to its feet. Together they walked across the camp. The hobbled dromedaries watched the man and the animal without emotion.

'A great misfortune, Caleb,' the padre said, looking in the dog's eyes for some sign of sympathy.

Major Porfirio unfolded the chair and sat outside his tent. He searched his pockets for the half-smoked cigar. The day was burning out. Over the hills an enormous red sun was setting. He observed it without thinking until a voice brought him back from his contemplation. His orderly was dressed in a pair of oversize breeches and a shirt with a buttoned-up collar that almost choked him. A towel hung down from his forearm – he had somewhere seen a waiter once carry one that way.

'Your meal is ready, major.'

Major Porfirio looked at him with affection.

'I'll have a glass of wine,' he said.

'I'm afraid there isn't any.'

The major frowned. He could remember that the last time he checked there were still several bottles left.

'That's true. But they've gone missing.'

The boy was a distant relative of his. When he was conscripted, his family had implored the major to keep him out of harm's way. Major Porfirio had interceded with the brigadier, and the boy was assigned to be their joint aide.

'I kept the bottles under my cot,' the orderly said. 'It must've happened the night I was in the infirmary.'

'The brigadier will be very troubled by this news,' Major Porfirio said.

He finished his cigar and received the tray with his meal. He lifted the tin covers and inspected every plate: a few slices of cornbread and a cup of thick soup. He skimmed off the crust of dirt in his cup and drank the lukewarm soup slowly, helping down each sip with a piece of cornbread. Interrupting his meal to swat the flies, he thought about the theft of the wine and the sugar. He was mystified by the fact that in such a desperate situation the men would concern themselves with profiteering.

He caught sight of Father Simeon walking across the camp with the dog, and he raised his hand in a greeting. Immediately the two silhouettes changed direction.

'Lost, Father?'

The padre nodded. 'In the labyrinth of sins. I run a church that has no congregation.'

'Don't blame them. They don't know whether they'll be alive tomorrow.'

'Even more so. The Lord can take away the fear.'

The major called to his orderly to bring the padre a chair. Father Simeon accepted it with thanks. As soon as he sat down, the dog crawled under it.

'If dogs could talk,' the padre said, 'they would teach the world humility.'

The dog beat the dust with its tail. Major Porfirio turned

17

his head and looked at the animal. He could not think of it as a creature in possession of moral superiority. He did marvel at its instinct to treat evil merely as a natural occurrence: something that one could not prevent but which one could run away from. He pushed back his cap and prepared to watch the sunset. The air was warm and silent, with a velvet texture. Next to the spectacle of his defeated troops, the beauty of the landscape seemed as inhuman as it was absolute. He contemplated with melancholy the sun burying itself in the earth.

'The fact of the matter is, Father, that this world would still be the same whether you and I were above ground or six feet under.' Night was coming. Above their heads the birds hurried away. 'I would offer you a glass of wine if only I knew who had the bottle.'

'Oh.' The padre twisted a strand of his beard. 'Stolen?'

'If the brigadier catches the thief, he'll set him at twelve paces.'

The padre looked away. 'We ought not to let our personal grudges get in the way of our mercy. After all, what are a few bottles of wine . . .'

'You don't understand the rules of the army, Father.'

The padre made a face.

'Oh, the army. The army would be run better by the Ecumenical Patriarch.'

'You know, you've got a point there.'

Above their heads flies buzzed, invisible in the dusk. The major thought about the Crusades. Suddenly he clapped his hands and inspected his palms: a small red smear was on his fingers. He brushed his hands on his trousers.

'If you hear anything at confession,' he said, 'you will of course let the brigadier know?'

Father Simeon shook his head in refusal.

'The contents of a confession aren't to be disclosed. But I promise to try and dissuade the sinner with all my powers.'

18

The dog whined. Father Simeon stretched his arm and stroked it. Across the camp the fires burned, and the mules nickered in the corral. Beyond the hills the moon was rising. It was not long before the bugle would be sounding lights out.

2

The brigadier knelt down and looked at his correspondence scattered across the floor of the lorry. The letters and post-cards lying in the dirt made him sad as if they were a flock of dead doves. He sat on his cot again and began to smooth everything with patience, brushing off the dust with his palm. Outside soldiers and animals walked about in silence. In the dusk small fires began to appear across the camp. A little hope stirred in Brigadier Nestor's heart – perhaps they stood a chance after all. He opened a random envelope from the bundle on his lap, read a few of the words he almost knew by heart and at once remembered his wife.

They had first met at a Christmas ball thirty-four years earlier, in a hotel of the capital, and married six months later. It had been a marriage of peaceful routines. There had been the occasional liaison, of course. Brigadier Nestor shrugged his shoulders: it was impossible for a soldier away from home for such long periods not to succumb. But nothing of substance, ever. He would have told her about them if she had been capable of comprehending – but it was different for women, he understood. He had long since absolved himself. As he turned the page, a photograph fell out: a child dressed in a sailor suit, riding a tricycle: Brigadier Nestor's grandson. The old officer held it at arm's length for some time, squinting and smiling with pride before returning it to the envelope.

Finally he found the letter from his daughter, which

announced the terrible news. He confirmed the date of his wife's death from pneumonia: a year ago tomorrow. He had to arrange the memorial service. 'Orderly!' he shouted in the direction of the hatch, and when the boy appeared: 'Ask the padre to come and see me.'

As soon as his orderly left, he thought something smelt bad. He searched the back of the lorry but found nothing until he fell on his knees. Under his cot was a dead snake. The discovery felt like an omen. The snake lay in the dust, twisted in the shape of the numeral eight. The brigadier opened his trunk and used his sword to drag it out. Holding it up, skewered from the tail, he studied the patterns of its skin.

'Orderly!'

The hatch to the driver's cabin opened. When the soldier saw the snake, his eyes opened wide.

'Who did this?' the officer asked.

The young man shrugged.

'I have no idea, my brigadier.'

'It couldn't have died of natural causes,' Brigadier Nestor said. 'It's head is crushed.'

'Perhaps, my brigadier.'

'You didn't do this?'

'No, sir.'

Beyond the windscreen evening was falling across the wilderness: a few broad strokes of dark colour on a canvas left otherwise unfinished. Brigadier Nestor passed the snake to his orderly.

'I don't care what the Bible says about the Serpent. Don't kill snakes. Throw them out with the broom.'

He cleaned his sword and put it back in the trunk, under a stack of starched and ironed shirts which had lost their freshness. He locked both padlocks and sat at his desk. Buried under his maps were the pair of compasses, the ruler and a pencil as small as a cigarette end. In his breast pocket were his spectacles. 'Now,' he puffed and fixed the wires of his glasses

21

behind his ears, 'let's find out where the hell we are.' He licked the blunt tip of his pencil and started.

For some time he was absorbed in the calculations he did on the margin of the maps. He only had a break to fill his cup with coffee and search for the protractor. He sipped the bitter coffee with a sentimental craving for sugar. More than an hour later, he put down his pencil and read out the disappointing news.

'Three hundred and twenty-two yards west of our last position. Plus or minus eleven. We're moving in circles.'

He removed his spectacles, fixed his eyes on the leather holster hanging over his head and recalled the legend of Damocles' sword.

'And we are headed away from the coast,' he added.

A gentle voice from outside brought him back:

'I could come back later.'

Brigadier Nestor waved the padre in.

'Come in, Father. My job won't be any easier in an hour or even a day.'

The padre climbed into the back of the lorry and started talking in a pleasant manner. He apologised for being late; it was because that afternoon he had caught a soldier eating corned beef. Brigadier Nestor looked at the padre with weary eyes.

'Is that an offence now?'

'Eating meat on Wednesday,' the padre explained.

Brigadier Nestor contemplated the map. There was a sweat stain where his palm had lain. He would have called the war a waste of time if it were not for the dead, the dispossessed, the refugees. No: it had been a catastrophe. Father Simeon was still talking.

'What is the point of fasting if not acquiring discipline. I had to produce the tin during confession to stop him denying it, my brigadier. It took me more than an hour to absolve him.'

'An hour, eh?'

Brigadier Nestor left his desk and lay on his cot. After a while he suspected that Father Simeon must have asked something because he had turned silent.

'Excuse me, Father, did you say something? I didn't hear you.'

The padre repeated his question.

'You wanted to see me?'

The brigadier tried to remember.

'Mm, yes. I need your services, Father.'

'A confession?'

The padre leaned forward. He was like a thirsty man bending down to drink from a tap. Brigadier Nestor scratched his head.

'It's too soon for that,' he said. 'Perhaps when all this is over.'

He reminded the padre that it was a year since his wife's death. The padre offered his condolences.

'A memorial service perhaps?' the officer asked.

'By all means, my brigadier.'

Brigadier Nestor thanked him and added, 'I should have been by her side.'

'How could you have been, my brigadier?'

'I know. This war . . .'

'Everyone has a cross to bear,' said the padre.

'At my age I shouldn't be bearing weights, Father.'

'It's a steep ascent to Calvary.'

The brigadier chuckled bitterly.

'The ascent I don't mind, Father. It's the crucifixion afterwards.'

The man of God could offer little more than a smile.

'It's natural to be afraid. But salvation could be round the corner.'

'There are no corners in the Field of Blood.'

Father Simeon took out his bible and riffled through it. '*Touching the Almighty, we cannot find him out*,' he read out. '*He is excellent in power, and in judgement, and in plenty of justice.*'

The flame in the lamp on the desk flickered. Brigadier Nestor said, 'One of these days, Father, you have to explain to me that whole lily business.'

Father Simeon frowned.

'The lily?'

'The lily of the Annunciation. Just how on earth—?'

'A miracle, my brigadier. It was a miracle.'

The officer nodded.

'A miracle. I see. Exactly what we need now.'

The padre stood up and turned to leave, but the brigadier spoke up again.

'Is it a sin to kill a snake, Father?'

'If it were going to harm you I should think not. Isn't it . . . the same in battle?'

'Yes, I like to think it is. Thank you, Father.'

They shook hands. Soon the padre was walking across the camp. His shoulders sloped under his army coat, and the cross on his chest swung from side to side. The dog was lying at the entrance to his tent, waiting for him. Father Simeon did not let it in. He pulled down the flap and went and sat on the edge of his cot. If only people trusted in God, he thought. Maybe that was the reason they had lost the war: the enemy had a blind faith in Allah and was not afraid of death. The enemy truly believed in Paradise – his own paradise, a barbaric notion, of course. He wondered: how many of the Christian soldiers believed in salvation? He looked at a coil of rope on the floor and remembered the conversation about the snake.

'God save us from the Serpent,' he said.

He lit a candle. Slowly a foul smell filled the air: ever since the paraffin had run out, he had been making candles from cattle fat. He wrapped himself in a blanket, and his eyes wandered across the wooden altarpiece. On it was a John the Baptist, a Saint George on horseback and an Entry into

24

Jerusalem where Jesus' donkey had the padre's face. It had been meant as an innocent jest, perhaps even as an exercise in humility, but the humorous painting now seemed a sanctimonious act. Father Simeon thought again about his religious failings and those of his congregation.

'Science,' he said unexpectedly.

His face reddened, and he stood up. With his hands made into fists, he paced his tent, head bent, mumbling. Science was the new religion in the Western world, he thought. The vainglory of professors, the grandiosity of lecture theatres, the doctrinal language of scientific treatises: how did those people dare challenge faith? He had seen photographs of laboratories, and it had struck him how much they resembled medieval torture chambers – the preposterousness of it all. Take for example the ridiculous theories of that German Zionist. He scratched his head, trying to remember the physicist's name in the newspaper not long ago.

'*Enistan*,' he said like a profanity. Yes. That man was becoming more popular than the other enemy of Orthodoxy, the Catholic scoundrel, the Pope. Father Simeon clasped his hands behind his back and continued to pace round the sombre religious objects. 'It only goes to prove that science is the Trojan Horse of the Jews,' he said. He was feeling out of his depth. The frustration of not knowing exactly what he was talking about only fuelled his vexation. 'The Enlightenment,' he said scornfully, twisting the tip of his beard. 'The scourge of Logic.' The fortunate Ottomans had missed all that. Father Simeon curled his lip. '*Blessed are the poor in spirit*,' he said. '*For theirs is the kingdom of heaven.*' He bowed his head and added with despair, 'As for us, we'll simply burn in Hell.'

The rows of stacked rifles gleamed in the twilight and in the glow of the campfires. Sitting cross-legged on a Muslim prayer rug, the corporal studied the chessboard. He rubbed the stubble on his chin and made brief sounds with his nose. The cold of the night was spreading across the camp; it would soon be impossible to stay outside. He wrapped himself tighter in his coat. The small square rug he sat on had tassels, a tendril design and an inscription in Arabic. The corporal never let it out of his sight. In violation of the orders that forbade looting, he had taken it from a house in an abandoned village the brigade had come to almost a year earlier. The rug was intended as a present for a special person back home. On the other side of the chessboard, the medic gave him an impatient look.

'Let me remind you that we're still playing. If I didn't know you were Christian, I would assume you were praying to Allah.'

The wind blew the smoke from the coffee pots in their direction. It was a smoke without aroma: the coffee had been cut with chicory. The corporal moved his bishop.

'Not there,' the medic said. 'The black square.'

'Which one?'

'Next to the pawn.'

'Right.' The corporal thought for a moment. 'No. Let me think.'

He took back his piece and rested his chin on his hand again. The medic left the game in order to urinate. When he returned the corporal was putting the pieces away.

'Let's play draughts,' he said. 'It's a democratic game where all the pieces start as equals.'

The medic made a gesture of indifference. His puttees were soiled, his tunic was missing its buttons, the stitching of his sleeve was coming apart at the shoulder. His temperament did not agree with his clothes. None of the horror and disenchantment of the war seemed to have affected him. He was like a judge presiding over the trial of a horrific crime: fascinated with the case and just. A medical student who had suspended his studies in order to join the army, he was no

26

political animal. In fact he would have been indifferent to the Cause if he knew what it was. His aim was to gain experience in shoestring surgery, which he planned to practise after the war in the remote parts of the homeland. Medicine was his religion and politics, and he wished to attend to it like a hermit. He treated friends and foes the same, in defiance of the rule that priority should be given to one's own casualties, an attitude that had earned him the public disapproval of his comrades.

'I've been meaning to ask you,' the corporal said. 'Last spring, why did you order the military police to cordon off that brothel?'

The medic frowned. During that incident he had had to threaten the soldiers with a loaded pistol to stop them from entering the house.

'That place was a conservatory of every disease suffered by man below the waist.'

'Would you have fired that gun?'

The medic spoke with a calmness that left no doubt.

'I'd kill in order to save life.'

The call of the bugle ended their game. The medic gathered the board and the draughtsmen and headed for the infirmary, a large round tent pitched in the middle of the camp with red crosses painted on its roof. Its sides were covered with paintings of wild animals, laughing clowns and acrobats in mid-air. The tent had been abandoned by an Armenian circus. He heard whining behind him. He bent down and examined the padre's dog. '*Alopecia areata*,' he said and patted the animal on the head. Caleb wagged his tail and sat down to scratch himself. The medic went to make his rounds.

Immediately he entered the circus tent, he smelt the antiseptic. He walked among the beds. One soldier had a bandaged head, another had his leg in a plaster cast, a third had his face buried under layers of compresses. Here and there the medic stopped briefly to examine a patient. He

27

pressed his palm on someone's forehead and nodded with satisfaction. When he held up another's wrist and felt his pulse, he screwed up his face, lifted a dressing soaked in pus and studied the wound. A nurse came up to him.

'Gangrene,' the medic said. 'Amputation first thing in the morning.'

The nurse, a big man with a child's smile, nodded respectfully. Before the war he had been a sponge fisher and had suffered the bends many times. He had hoped to enlist in the navy but had not been given the choice: the infantry had a greater need for men. He had served under the medic from the start of the campaign.

'I'll sterilise the tools,' he said.

Mosquitoes fell against the oil lamps that hung from the roof. The medic continued his rounds, giving more orders. He indicated which casts could be removed, pointed out the dirty bandages which had not yet been changed, reminded the nurse to place an order with the carpenter for splints. The nurse followed close behind with his hands in the pockets of his apron. His sleeves were rolled up, revealing an anchor tattoo on his forearm.

'There're some terminal cases, doctor,' he said. 'Perhaps we could save drugs . . .'

The medic pursed his lips.

'I'm not in charge of the firing squad,' he said.

'I only meant—'

'Never mind, nurse. I'll set up the laboratory.'

'We need sedatives, chloroform and aspirin.'

'And the philosopher's stone,' his superior said.

His quarters were in the next tent. They were furnished simply: a desk, a chair, a cot covered with a blanket. A cabinet with labelled drawers was the medical archive. Crates marked with the emblem of the International Red Cross took up the rest of the space. The medic sat on the chair with the intention of working but could not stay awake. He fell asleep and dreamed that he was in a big laboratory with high ceilings and rows of tables on which were laid beakers, glass tubes and precision scales. He wore a lab coat and was looking through a microscope. After a while a door opened, and an old man in a suit and bow tie walked in. He knew that face: the white beard, the large forehead, the grey hair. The man looked exactly like the photograph in his books: Louis Pasteur. He leaned over the bench.

'Well?'

The medic sighed.

'It's impossible, professor.'

'The germs, my son. Think of the glass of milk. The process of fermentation. Disease develops in a similar way.'

The medic looked through the microscope again.

'Such a small organism.'

The old scientist nodded.

'Quite. It can bring down a vastly larger one.'

'How can we beat it?'

'Inoculation. It worked with septicaemia, cholera, diphtheria, tuberculosis, smallpox, hydrophobia. And we're only at the start. There're many other applications.'

'But what about the war, professor?'

'The war? We haven't discovered the vaccine for that yet.'

'There is no vaccine against foolishness, professor.'

The old man shrugged.

'No? That's what they used to say about rabies too.'

The medic woke up from his dream with a sense of hope. But it began to fade in the sallow glow of the storm lantern on his desk and the grim, dark reality beyond. He did not believe in omens. What he believed in was in the crates round him, which contained the equipment of a rudimentary laboratory, a benefaction paid for by wealthy expatriates. He unpacked the chemicals and read the labels. He was careful with the Carl Zeiss microscope. He found a wall chart of the periodic table, spread it over his desk, turned up the lamp and sat down to study it.

A voice behind him said, 'The bugle called lights out an hour ago. You're in breach of the regulations.'

Major Porfirio stood with his thumbs hooked in his belt.

'You're fortunate I'm not the enemy,' he added. 'You could've had your throat slit.'

The medic gave him a weary glance.

'The enemy? I can't remember the last time I set eyes on the enemy. By now we must be a fairy tale to scare their children with.'

'The war isn't over.'

The medic returned to studying the periodic table.

'They call it the theatre of war,' he said after a while. 'But I think it rather resembles a circus.'

Major Porfirio remembered the reason for his visit.

'I need to borrow your razor. I seem to have misplaced mine.'

'Are you losing your beard?'

'The old man disapproves of it.'

The medic leaned over his desk and rolled up the periodic table. He looked for his cut-throat razor but could not find it anywhere.

'It was *there*,' he said. 'Right there. I always keep it between the shaving brush and the surgical spirit.'

Major Porfirio thought of the recent thefts of the sugar and the wine.

'When was the last time you used it?'

'Yesterday before we marched. But I'm sure it was there when I came in tonight.'

'Anyone come in?'

The medic nodded.

'Yes. Louis Pasteur.'

'Who?'

'No one. Just a dream. I dozed off.'

The two men stood in the middle of the tent, pouting and feeling powerless among the wooden Red Cross crates, in the weak yellow glow of the storm lantern.

The moon came out from behind the hills and rose above the plateau. The wind quietened, and the birds perched on the barren hills. Caleb walked across the camp. The air stood like sheets of glass. His breath puffed up from his snout, and his eyes moved from side to side with vigilance. His ears turned in the direction of a noise, and he lifted his muzzle and sniffed the air. His tail had lost its hair, and it now seemed as if he were dragging a piece of rope.

His disease was not the only instance of bad luck in his life. The day he was born, under a minaret in Istanbul, a refuse lorry had run over his mother. He had suckled another dog and grown to hunt rats and cats until a warden from the Board of Hygiene had caught him in his net. He was thrown in a ship with other strays and was carried across the Sea of Marmara to a small island off the Anatolian coast, where he was let loose to die of thirst and starvation. But no sooner had the funnel of the steamer disappeared than Caleb had entered the water. The Asian coastline had loomed several miles ahead. Behind him the other dogs had howled with fear and desperation. Many days later he had entered the town of Bursa all but dead from exhaustion. It was there that Father Simeon had come across him in the first year of the war.

Caleb stopped and scratched himself. When he finished he had another bald patch in his coat. Someone whistled, and the dog walked up to him and let him stroke him. But when the man shook a bone with some meat on it, Caleb walked away: he trusted only Father Simeon's hand to feed him. The stars had come out, and he raised his head. He whined with boredom – if only he had a companion. He yawned and let his tongue catch the moisture in the air. One of his incisors had rotted and fallen out. Outside the makeshift church, he sat down and rested his muzzle on the ground. Under the moonlight a squad of soldiers was heading for sentry duty.

The night passed slowly in the camp and over the hills. Some time later Caleb heard footsteps and saw a man approach. Immediately he stood up and began to snarl, but when the man came closer, he recognised his master. He tried to follow him into the tent, but the padre forbade it. For a while a murmur came from inside, where the shadow of Father Simeon wrapped in a blanket moved about. The candle went out, and only the glow of the brazier remained. A little while later, snoring began inside the tent.

3

Brigadier Nestor emerged from the makeshift church with his mood unchanged. Neither the mass commemorating his wife nor the early-morning shot of morphia had helped. He put on his cap and shook hands with Father Simeon, thanking him for his services. The sun had not yet appeared; a line of blue light grew across the horizon. The vultures had not arrived. The wind had quietened, and the earth was still cool. It was a brief moment of peace administered daily like medication, but it was a medicine that soothed rather than cured: the army remained lost. The brigadier contemplated the horizon while the preparations for the departure of the brigade continued. In any direction he turned, he saw no sign to suggest a way out of the labyrinth. Since Anatolia was east of the Aegean, they could go west and eventually reach the coast. But a journey across land was not a simple problem of plane geometry. What was the condition of the terrain ahead? Perhaps the sea was closer if they travelled south or southwest. And above all, where was the enemy at that moment? One thing was certain: they should not head east.

Brigadier Nestor found his compass and advised his orderly, who also drove his lorry, which direction to follow. Then he gave the signal to march. Slowly the column started. His lorry led the way, followed by the vehicles with the wounded, ammunition, food and water. Behind the motorcade the soldiers walked in silence. From an entire brigade at the beginning of the enemy offensive, there remained only

two incomplete infantry battalions, a company of *evzones**
dressed in skirts, a squadron of horsemen and an artillery
battery. Behind the troops came a long train of mules and
dromedaries, laden with more provisions.

The brigadier had slept little the previous night. At one
time he had dreamed of his wife, suspended an inch from the
floor, and later of the dead snake he had found under his cot.
During a stop to repair a tyre, Major Porfirio came to see him.
The brigadier saw that his subordinate had only clipped his
beard.

'I thought I made it clear a beard doesn't suit an officer,' he
said. 'If you're so fond of it, you should've joined the clergy.'

Major Porfirio reported the theft of the wine and the
razors. Outside, the orderly lifted the wheel of the lorry off
the ground with a jack. While he worked, the long column of
soldiers continued to pass by. As the lorry began to tilt to one
side, the two officers inside held on to the bars of the roof.
The table and the stove started to slide downwards. Brigadier
Nestor felt seasick. A bitter substance rose to his mouth, and
he had to swallow several times to stop himself from
vomiting. At last the jack stopped, and his mind returned to
the thefts.

'There's a time and place for everything,' he said. 'Thieving
is a peacetime pursuit. We have to keep our wits about us. If
these thefts continue, morale will deteriorate even more.
There's always the business of the handbills.'

Only two days earlier, the agitator had struck again. This
time the handbills had been more incendiary than ever before
in accusing the military and political leaders of being
responsible for the disaster. Brigadier Nestor had walked
across the camp shouting at his men not to touch them while
he frantically collected the handbills himself with a pair of
tweezers. It had been more than a symbolic gesture. In his

---

*Soldiers of an elite Greek infantry unit used as assault troops.

panic he had come up with a story in order to stop his troops from reading them: the agitator was an enemy spy who had daubed the paper with arsenic to inflict casualties.

'The only way to stop the troops from discussing what's written in those handbills would be to cut off their tongues,' he said.

'I could reopen the handbill inquiry,' Major Porfirio offered.

'No. From now on *I* will conduct all investigations. It'd give me something to do. Something to stop the heat from stewing my brain.'

When Brigadier Nestor was alone again, he took to his cot to rest, but the heat was suffocating. He decided to go for a walk. He climbed down off his lorry at the moment the cavalry squadron was passing by. Despite the slow pace of the horses, he was overwhelmed by the clamour of the hoofs, the stirrups and the sabres hanging from the side of the saddles. He stood frozen with fear. It was the corporal who brought him back from his stupor.

'Be careful, my brigadier. My horse has a grudge against the army.'

He was riding a chestnut gelding with white shins and a cropped mane. Brigadier Nestor raised his head and gave the animal an inquisitive look.

'He'll never forgive me for depriving him of his virility,' the corporal said.

The horse snorted and shook its head from side to side. It had long deep scars across its neck and croup: they were lash marks. The brigadier felt pity for the animal. He caressed its forelock.

'Sometimes I, too, feel like a eunuch,' he said. 'At my age, even mandrake does not work.' He pointed at the scars. 'What are these for?'

The corporal looked at the horse indifferently.

'Oh, he threw me off. One of these days he'll snap my neck.'

He saluted and rejoined his comrades. Some had an arm in a sling or their head wrapped in bandages, which were caked with blood. Others were missing an entire limb. Watching them Brigadier Nestor felt again the weight of his responsibility for keeping them alive. He removed his kepi and wiped his forehead with the back of his hand. It was nearly midday, and the heat hung in the air like drapery. He held his hand above his eyes to shield them from the sun and surveyed the landscape. Beyond the hills he spotted some ruins. Was it an ancient temple? The Anatolian land was littered with them: they were the scattered pages of a book no one wished to read.

He recalled when the army had been ordered to build fortifications in order to defend some town from the attacks of the enemy. Not far away there had been an Alexandrian citadel. The officers had entered through a crack in the wall and walked around admiring the columns, the friezes and mouldings of the defunct city. A copse of fig trees had grown among the ruins. Brigadier Nestor had ordered his cartographers to sketch everything for the benefit of future historians before giving, with a pain in his heart, the order to dynamite the place so that they could use the stones to fortify the nearby town.

His orderly finished changing the tyre and lowered the jack. Up ahead, the brigade had moved on. Brigadier Nestor headed back to his lorry.

'What a torment,' he said. 'Being the captain of the Ship of Fools.'

Not long after, the column stopped again at a well: a low wall of stones placed on top of each other, a pulley on the end of a pole, a rope hooked on to a goatskin. The brigadier leaned over the hole and shouted through his cupped hands: 'King Midas has ass's ears!' A fading echo repeated his words down the dry shaft. He raised his head and contemplated the plain with watery eyes. Father Simeon walked past with a tin megaphone.

'You spend too much time in the sun, Father,' the brigadier said. 'You'll get sunstroke. You're crazy.'

The padre smiled.

'That's what they used to tell Saint John the Baptist.'

The two men stood under the sun like numbers in an equation that has no solution. Brigadier Nestor thought, it was a stroke of genius to found a religion on the embrace of earthly suffering: no promise needed to be fulfilled in this life. He tried to think of faiths that actually exhorted carnal desire. If they ever existed, had they survived – or would they – as long as Judaism, Christianity or Islam? The column of men, animals and lorries went noisily by.

'Do me a favour, Father. Get in the shade. You can have your head served on a platter when I'm not in command any more.'

'Life these days gives a priest very few chances to prove his faith,' the padre said.

But he obeyed. Watching him climb into the back of a lorry, the brigadier had a premonition. He looked around him. Propped up against a tree was the old postman's motorcycle his Chief of Staff had requisitioned after the death of his horse; Major Porfirio was shaving in the shade. The brigadier searched for a sign that something was wrong. The landscape offered him nothing out of the ordinary, but he was convinced something unusual was about to happen – he only wondered whether it would be good or evil. Still thinking about it, he went to see the medic. He found him having his meal alone in his Red Cross lorry. When he saw him, the medic wiped his lips on his sleeve.

'My brigadier.'

The old man waved him at ease.

'I hope I've arrived in surgery hours,' the brigadier said.

'There'll come a time when people will get sick only when us doctors tell them to. Until then we stay open all day.'

The brigadier removed his cap and climbed into the lorry.

37

'Please, finish your meal, doctor. I can wait.' He turned the rear-view mirror towards him, wiped off the dust and looked at his reflection. 'One day, you doctors will be able to raise the dead too,' he said and ran his fingers through his hair. 'But you still won't have found a cure for baldness.'

'Oh, that matter will be settled by the process of natural selection,' the medic said.

He broke a piece of hardtack, dipped it in his soup and chewed it slowly. He was a man at ease with his conscience but not a Pharisee. He knew the limitations of his character and abilities and also knew he was doing his best under the circumstances: he was not responsible for the ugliness of the world. The brigadier unbuttoned his tunic and breathed out with relief. That morning his orderly had brushed his uniform, sewn back the shoulder straps, darned the holes in the pockets and polished his boots. The brigadier had not noticed until now.

'Hell,' he said. 'For a moment I thought I was wearing someone else's uniform.'

The medic looked up from his mess tin.

'It could've been worse. To think you were someone else wearing your uniform. Do you want your blood pressure taken?'

The sun moved a little, and the cabin was flooded with light.

'Pressure? No, no. I just need a little morphia.'

The medic was surprised that the secret that their commanding officer was addicted to the drug had not yet been revealed to the soldiers by the handbills. He nodded.

'How much, brigadier?'

His superior requested an enormous amount.

'That could kill an elephant,' the medic said.

By now the old man admitted that he was a regular user but still denied he was an addict. In the past he had obtained his medicine from civilian pharmacists, but the brigade had not been near a town for over a week. He promised the medic that as soon as things improved he would give it up. He said, 'I tried camomile infusions to calm me down, but they don't work.' The medic accepted the argument. He thought, how could one remain sane when everything was falling apart? He knew little about insanity: the barred ward, the soiled gowns, the obscenities. He refused to imagine his commanding officer in that world. He left the lorry and returned a moment later with a large bottle. The brigadier remembered the other reason for his visit.

'I understand you've been the victim of a theft,' he said.

'The razor? It wasn't of any value. I can shave with a scalpel.'

'Any idea who took it?'

'Could be anyone. I was asleep at the time. Oh, it's not important.'

The brigadier hitched up the bottle under his arm and opened the door of the lorry.

'Nevertheless,' he said, 'it's another link in a chain of worrying incidents.'

Outside he had that premonition again. He looked around him but, again, saw nothing strange: only lorries, horses, dromedaries, artillery guns. Dazed by the sun, the soldiers marched on. He squeezed the morphia bottle under his arm and took a deep breath. He looked for his lorry and saw it at the head of the column, way ahead. Without warning his knees started to give. He heard the beating of his heart as if it were coming from far away. His eyes stung. Everything appeared as if he were looking at it from behind a tinted glass. He tried to breathe, but his chest deflated like a balloon. He felt tired; he had to have his shot. The morphia bottle slipped from under his arm, and he bent down to pick it up. He could not stand the heat. His carotids throbbed. The last thing he remembered before losing consciousness was someone grabbing hold of him by the arms and lifting him up from the burning earth.

Major Porfirio wiped the blade on his shirtsleeve and folded the borrowed razor. For a brief moment, he looked at his reflection in the mirror and then brushed his tunic and put it on. He sat on his motorcycle and began to pedal. The motor gave no sign of starting up. A moment later he stopped and caught his breath under the shadow of the tree.

At first he heard a distant neighing but thought nothing of it. Then he recognised the rhythmic crack of a whip. He sat up on the footrests of his motorcycle and studied the landscape all round while the whipping continued mercilessly. In the distance he saw the dark shape of a creature with a human upper body but the lower body and legs of a horse. Major Porfirio jumped off the motorcycle and walked towards it. It was a soldier whipping a horse. Every time the whip came down, the major felt a pang of anger. The corporal held his horse by the reins and was whipping it with his cartridge belt. He was panting. There was blood on his forehead. The blood mixed with his sweat and trickled down his cheeks.

'Stop that,' the major said.

The corporal looked up and grinned: in a flash the martyr's bleeding face gave way to a murderer's. Major Porfirio had seen it all before in war when the coin was tossed, and no one could guess which side it would land: humanity or brutality. He suddenly remembered the massacre of the civilians.

'Enough,' he said.

'Major?'

The corporal had not heard. He raised the belt and brought it down on the horse's back with force again. The major grabbed his arm.

'I said, *stop*.'

The corporal looked at him with surprise.

'I'm sorry, my major. Did you say something?'

'What's the meaning of this, corporal?'

The horse shook with fear. It twisted its neck, snorting and breathing fast. There were deep cuts on its back and it was bleeding.

'It almost killed me, major,' the corporal said and pointed at his forehead.

'Fool,' the officer said through clenched teeth.

'It's only a horse, major.'

In the trees the cicadas stopped buzzing, without a reason. The officer looked at the horizon: there was nothing there. The horse tried to free itself, but the corporal held its reins tightly.

'It's army property,' the major said. 'If I see you doing this again, you'll make the rest of the journey on foot.'

'Yes, major.'

'I'm disappointed in you, corporal.'

'It's only a horse, major.'

'Go.'

The corporal pulled the horse away in silence, and the major returned to his motorcycle. He started to pedal, and the cicadas started again. He took hold of the handlebars, opened the throttle and managed to start the motorcycle. For some time he revved the engine then put on his goggles and set off.

The lunar landscape extended as far as he could see. When he caught up with the column, he heard the padre in the back of a lorry speaking through his megaphone. That day he was reading from Deuteronomy:

'. . . *The Lord your God which goeth before you, He shall fight for you, according to all that He did for you in Egypt before your eyes. And in the wilderness, where thou hast seen how that the Lord my God bare thee, as a man doth bear his son, in all the way that ye went, until ye came into this place . . .*'

The troops marched silently in the sun, paying no attention

to the sermon. Major Porfirio raised his eyes to the sky and contemplated a swarm of cormorants almost with jealousy. Then he lowered his head to the plateau and thought about the injured horse.

Inside his lorry Brigadier Nestor was recovering from the sunstroke. He lifted the lid of the pot and watched the syringe sink slowly into the bubbling water. He covered the pot and sat down at his desk. In front of him were the maps. He propped his head against his arm and gave them a brief, impatient look. They were covered with lines drawn in pencil, each a little further inland from the Aegean coast like beach marks left by the tide: the front at different stages of the expedition. Where was he the day his wife had passed on? He could not remember. He turned one of the maps round and on the back drew two columns with his pencil. One he labelled *Name of suspect* and the other *Piece of evidence*, then he started filling them in. He had not worked for long when he felt his throat dry. He stopped, poured himself a glass of water and gulped it. It was warm and gave him little release from his thirst – he would give anything now for a block of ice. He did not have another glass but reached for the pot. He had just rolled up his sleeve when he heard shouting from outside. With the syringe in his hand, he moved the flap aside, and when his eyes adjusted to the glare of the afternoon sun, he saw at last the reason for his premonition.

4

Air Lieutenant Kimon rested his elbows on the edge of the cockpit and surveyed the ground with his binoculars. He was always happy when he was flying; the air at that altitude was cool and clear. The shadow of his biplane rippled over the saltpetre hills. Flying seemed to Air Lieutenant Kimon not dissimilar to swimming underwater, where the only sound one could hear was one's own breathing: in the air it was the noise of the engine. Had he been afraid of heights, he would be a deep-sea diver.

For a while he searched the terrain. Then he put away his binoculars and removed his helmet. The wind blasted his forehead and hair. Keeping his eyes shut, he experienced a brief moment of exuberance as if he were not on a military mission but an aerobatics display. He wished he could take part in an air show. After the war he wanted to buy his own aeroplane and travel across Europe performing stunts with a flying circus. He covered his head again and turned up the throttle. The exhaust pipe backfired and petrol sprayed his face. Rocking from side to side, the biplane raced ahead.

He had taken off that morning on a reconnaissance mission to look for survivors of the defeat. He had been searching for several hours but found nothing. It was one month since the collapse of the front: if there were any troops alive, they would have been captured by the enemy. But he followed his orders.

He saw he was headed for a stratus cloud. He pushed the

control column, and the biplane began to descend. The air became warmer and immediately he thought he was flying too low. No sooner had he cleared the cloud than he was caught in a whirlwind. He only had time to cover his mouth and nose with his scarf before the biplane plunged into the column of spinning dust. He grabbed the steering column with both hands and pulled it back. Buried in the whirlwind, he could see nothing but felt the plane being pulled down, pushed sideways then let climb higher.

It lasted only a minute, and then the biplane came out of the darkness. Air Lieutenant Kimon cleared his goggles and inspected the damage. The dirt inside the cockpit was up to his knees, and the fabric of the wings had holes in it, but all the struts and wires seemed intact. He looked over his shoulder: the rudder was slightly bent, but worked. Then the engine started to knock, and at once he knew the dust had choked the carburettor. A moment later the engine stalled altogether, and the biplane began to lose altitude.

Father Simeon screwed up his eyes. Something had caught the dog's attention. He followed the animal to the top of a hill with a prickling sensation at the nape of his neck. When he reached the ridge of the hill, he stopped to catch his breath. He shielded his eyes, checked his panting and saw it.

The yellow biplane passed overhead. Father Simeon made out its silver nose, the struts of its wings, the blue-and-white cross painted on its tail. He had once been invited to bless a squadron and sprinkle the aeroplanes with holy water for good luck. Afterwards he and the other guests had watched a display of takeoffs, landings and manoeuvres. What had impressed him more than the antics of the pilots had been the infernal noise – but the aeroplane above his head was as quiet as a leaf. The yellow biplane circled the camp, looking for level ground to land.

Soon everyone had noticed. The soldiers dropped their

mess tins, left behind their boots and ran towards the descending speck, shouting and waving with joy. They made it to the place the pilot had chosen as his landing strip the moment the biplane touched down. But with its engine cut, it was descending too fast. Its wheels sank in the dirt, and it turned over. There was silence that lasted only a moment because then there was a large explosion, and the biplane went up in flames.

The soldiers rushed to the wreck. They pulled out the airman and carried him to safety. They removed his goggles, his helmet and the jacket that was singed by the flames and waited for the medic to arrive. He came with his first-aid box: nothing more than a bottle of ether, one of pure alcohol, a wad of cotton and some stained bandages that had been washed several times over. It was like a priest's portable altarpiece: it had more of a symbolic than a remedial value. He held the ether under the pilot's nostrils until the airman opened his eyes and took a deep breath. He looked around him with confused eyes. Not far away his biplane burned with a bright red fire and a dense billow of smoke.

Despite the medic's attempts to dissuade him, the airman insisted on being helped to his feet. When he stood up, he asked for a drink, and they handed him a water bottle. The water trickled down his gullet, blistered by the fumes he had inhaled during the accident, and caused more pain than relief. While he drank, Brigadier Nestor's voice was heard in the crowd: 'Out of my way.' The soldiers moved aside to let him through, and soon the old man appeared, dressed in his vest and breeches. Confronted with the burning wreck, he pushed back his cap and watched it in silence. Then he turned to the airman and gave him an irritated look.

'What news of the withdrawal, lieutenant?'

The airman finished the water before he spoke.

'It's over, sir. They are discussing the terms of the armistice now. This was meant to be my last mission.'

The brigadier turned and looked at the fire again.

'It is.'

The smoke rose thick and black in the air, attracting the vultures. They flew in circles around it, intrigued by the chips of wood and shreds of fabric carried away by the wind. The smoke passed in front of the sun, and Brigadier Nestor's disappointment eclipsed his anger.

'That's it,' he said. 'I can almost hear them back home singing our dirges.'

Father Simeon put on his cross and opened his bible. Its spine was broken, the cover was torn and all of Genesis and half of Exodus were missing. The damage had not only been a sin but also a cause for personal disappointment to him: it was Caleb who had done it. After seven days of sulking, the padre had forgiven him.

Caps were removed and heads bowed. Slowly the flames died down. All that remained of the biplane was its charred frame. Father Simeon leafed through the bible, took a deep breath and started. While he read a rain of ash began to fall over the camp, settling on the kepis of the men, their shoulders, the pages of the bible, Father Simeon's beard. It fell throughout the recitation of the Gospel and was still falling when, some time later, while the congregation was singing a psalm, the airman touched his forehead, went pale and collapsed with a thud on to the dust that was peppered with ash.

The medic passed the time of the brief afternoon halt for rest and repairs in the Red Cross lorry with a stack of old medical journals. He read lying on the floor, occasionally turning back a few pages to verify the data in a chart. There was a deep cut in his cheek from the scalpel he had used to shave. The interior of the lorry, which had no windows, was lit by the glow of the sun through the canvas. He heard the flap being raised but did not take his eyes from the article.

'Anything interesting?' the padre asked.

The medic turned the page.

'Hardly. These journals date from the time of Hippocrates.'

Father Simeon sat on a stool and removed his skullcap. Outside, hot gusts of air pushed against the taut fabric of the tent. The padre folded his cap in two and mopped the sweat on his forehead.

'In the old times, medicine and religion were inseparable,' he said.

Lying on his back, the medic dropped the journal to the floor and lifted another from the pile.

'But the average life span at that time was half of what is today,' he said. He bent back the cover, and a cloud of dust sprinkled his face: the beetles had been eating his archive. 'This was a case study of acute appendicitis,' he said.

The padre talked about the handbills.

'One of these days they will catch the traitor who circulates them.'

'Ever since the thefts began, the brigadier has forgotten all about them,' the medic said.

The padre suffered from the heat. His gaze moved round the interior of the tent, but nothing caught his attention.

He asked, 'How's the man who fell from the skies?'

'He'll have a bad headache when he wakes up and might suffer from amnesia.'

'Amnesia,' repeated the padre. 'There're certain things I wish I'd forgotten myself.'

The medic knew he was referring to the massacre.

'Whether you remember them or not, Father, those things did happen.'

'A sin not confessed is a yoke across the shoulders,' the padre said.

'We're swimming in a sea of sins and you're worried it might rain?'

'Every evening I wait in church for someone to come to confession . . .'

47

'Have you at least absolved yourself?'

Father Simeon heard the dog bark in the infernal afternoon – probably at a vulture. The stench of his sweat and the smell of disinfectant on the medic's clothes added to his misery. While he thought of Hell, the shapes of soldiers appeared on the canvas of the lorry like puppets in a shadow play. An unresolved feeling came over him. The medic lowered the journal and observed him with his medical eyes.

'Funeral rites wouldn't have done them any good,' the padre said. 'They weren't Christians.'

'Better forget it. Even you can't raise the dead, Father.'

Father Simeon stood up to leave.

'Maybe this misfortune has something to do with divine justice.'

The crumpled shoulder straps of his uniform were braided with the emblem of his eternal faith, the Christian cross. There was a hint of pleading in what he had just said. He yearned for someone to agree with him. The man lying on the floor denied him that consolation.

'Or with a broken compass,' the medic retorted.

After leaving the medic's quarters, the padre wandered along the column. The brightness of the earth dazed him. He walked unsteadily, obliviously, headachy. He shielded his eyes with his hand and surveyed the landscape. Some ragged tents were pitched in neat rows, lorries were parked in straight lines, smoke was rising from the stack of the field kitchen. It was like a small forgotten town that existed in a precarious transience, a place which an imminent natural disaster was about to wipe out: no one would notice. He resumed his walk. Anywhere else such silence would be unnatural for such a large gathering: it was the curfew of the heat. Father Simeon surprised a vulture wandering about with a limp.

He remembered with longing his house in a small village lost in the mountains: a single-storey house made of stone, with a tiled roof and a small veranda. It was an image of peace and solitude: he had not married. It was neither a coincidence nor self-reliance that had made him decide not to. After cancelling his plans to become a missionary, he had nurtured the ambition of training for the office of bishop instead. To achieve it he had to preserve his celibacy. His old unfulfilled aspiration now seemed haughty to him.

He thought more of home. He compared the permanence of his old stone church to the flimsiness of his makeshift chapel here in Anatolia, and for the first time since the landing he understood how impossible the task of the Expeditionary Corps had been: after all, they were invaders. He thought, one after another the old empires dissipated, slowly but inexorably: the French, the Habsburgs, the Ottomans. Yet the motherland had gone to war, looking back with desire to her own long-gone imperial past. He came across Brigadier Nestor's orderly filling a radiator. The boy looked up. Deep in his thoughts, the padre made the sign of the cross in his direction and carried on.

The sight of his tent intensified his glum feelings. He had set it up in case anyone wanted to pray, but there was no one about. The wind had loosened the ropes, and the tarpaulin was slack and covered in dirt. The wooden cross on the roof was tilted to one side. Inside, the draught had toppled the altarpiece and covered it with dirt. For a while Father Simeon surrendered himself to the spectacle and then started tidying up. He fetched a spade and carried out the dirt, took off the sheet from his cot and cleaned it, then raised the altarpiece and wiped it. Last he swept the rugs. Once everything was in order again, he undressed and lay down on his cot.

At least it was cool inside his tent. The altarpiece cut down some of the glare of the sun through the canvas. A cloud of flies circled over his head. He breathed forcibly and quickly, in little puffs. He was tired. He closed his eyes, but the dust in the air was making him sneeze. Soon he abandoned his efforts

49

to sleep and lay with his hands folded under his head, observing the flies. He could no longer avoid thinking about the massacre.

It had happened more than two years earlier. He recalled the entry of the brigade, fresh from a bloody but ultimately won battle, into the small town. A long time had passed, but the place appeared in his memory clearly: the mannequin in the tailor's window, the striped pole outside a barbershop, the fountain in the square. In a battle that had taken place not far from the town, the enemy bombs had hit the artillery batteries of the brigade with unusual accuracy. Several times Brigadier Nestor had ordered them moved, but they still could not escape the deadly shelling: someone had been giving away the position of the guns. In the small town, the padre had watched nervously while the soldiers searched every house. It was not long before they had discovered the telephone which they assumed had been used to inform the enemy.

There were tamarisks in the square where they had herded the people, round the dry fountain. No one had admitted guilt during the inquiry. The shooting had lasted a long time – the square was too small to line up more than a dozen people at one time. Father Simeon had watched without emotion. The ordeal of the battle had affected him too. How could he have done nothing to prevent the murder? Lying on his cot, he felt his eyes water and covered his face with his forearm. He felt the tingling of a fly on his wrist. Somewhere someone was trying to start an engine.

Standing a few yards away, a vulture flapped its wings a couple of times and watched the orderly. After several attempts, the boy let go of the crank and wiped his forehead.

'The padre ought to write a prayer for the starting of internal combustion engines,' he said.

He lifted the bonnet and unscrewed the spark plugs,

cleaned each with a steel brush, bent their electrodes and placed them back. He went to the front and grabbed the crank again.

'In the name of the Father, and of the Son and of the Holy Ghost,' he said.

He gave the handle a yank. This time the engine sprang to life. Frightened by the noise, the vulture took flight and began to circle the camp. Turning its naked head with the enormous bill from side to side, it inspected the humans and the draught animals. It was evening. Another day had passed in which the bird had to eat from the rubbish heap. It wondered whether following the troops had been the right decision. The long shadow of the flagpole in the middle of the camp fell on a row of tents and faded over the dirt. Other birds joined the vulture and croaked a greeting. The vulture did not reply; it was eyeing a large round tent with red crosses on the canvas from where a delicious smell was rising. It had almost forgotten the smell of fresh blood. Now that the war was over, they would begin to bury the dead again. The vulture did not understand war. All it knew was that after three good years it was once more hard to find carrion. It croaked back at the other birds, but it sounded more like a curse than a greeting.

The orderly raised his eyes to the sky and gave the bird a brief look. He opened the door of the lorry and threw the crank on the seat. He took out a stethoscope from his pocket and listened at the engine. Happy with the sound of the valves, he lowered the bonnet, turned off the engine and cleaned his hands on his trousers. Soon the brigadier would rise from his afternoon nap, and he had to have his coffee ready.

He climbed on the back of the lorry, where he took the lid off the tin and saw that the coffee was running out. He poured in some chicory and shook the tin. Then he stirred two spoonfuls of the mix in the water and lit the fire under the pot. He opened the trunk to take out the sugar but then

51

remembered it had been stolen. Lifting the pot and putting it down again, he let the coffee boil three times before taking it off the fire. He poured the coffee in a cup, placed the cup on a saucer, filled a glass with fresh water and put everything on a tray. There was only one more thing he always served his commanding officer together with his coffee, and he stretched his arm under the bed. Casual at first, his expression soon changed to one of concern, and then to panic. He dropped to his knees and made a furious search.

Some time later he was entering his commanding officer's tent with a slight tremble and a lump in his throat. Somehow he had to break the news to him that his box of cigars had also disappeared.

The old circus tent glowed in the sun. Inside, the temperature rose steadily. After travelling in circles for two days, the brigade had halted and scouts had been sent out. They had been gone for a day already, which was enough time to pitch the tent of the infirmary and look after the wounded. The sun cast the shadows of the red crosses and animals painted on the canvas over the earthen floor and the cots. They were like projections of a children's carousel lamp: the dark silhouette of a prancing tiger with sabre claws, an elephant with a raised trunk, a cobra dancing to a charmer's flute, a kangaroo wearing boxing gloves. Hitched to the foot of every cot was a progress chart that showed a flat curve. A drip hung next to each patient. It should have represented hope, the possibility of recovery; instead it stood like a rudimentary cross above a shallow grave. In one of the beds a soldier with his head wrapped in bandages was trying to understand his progress chart. After a while he held it up. He asked, 'Can anyone explain this to me?'

A man with his leg in a cast sat up, put on his glasses and squinted at the chart across the aisle. 'If that monitored stock price,' he said, 'I would advise you to sell.'

A few cots away the airman slept quietly with a water pouch on his head. His face bore the signs of mixed lineage: light brown skin, blond hair and blue eyes. It was obvious to everyone in the infirmary that he was an aristocrat.

His father, a man from Alexandria and widower of a

foreign beauty, had never remarried but devoted his life to the trade of cotton, with offices in Piraeus, Marseilles and Manchester. The boy had a lonely childhood of sailor suits and garden mazes, boarding-schools and obligatory pastimes: piano lessons, fencing, equitation. He was a student of classics in Vienna when, during a long walk in the Prater, he had chanced upon the landing of a triplane on a daisy field. The noise of the engine and the soot of its exhaust had immediately won him over from lyric poetry. Some time later the Anatolian expedition had been announced, and he had returned home to volunteer for the Air Corps, a decision taken more out of his love of flying than patriotic fervour. All his father's connections could achieve was for the air lieutenant to be posted to a reconnaissance unit and not a raid squadron.

When he opened his eyes, a big man in a white apron looked down at him. The nurse held up a trephine and grinned. Air Lieutenant Kimon tried but could not speak. Where was he? The other patients snored, and a spade dug far away. He thought of a grave and a body thrown into it – no coffin, no shroud. His dizziness let only morbid thoughts filter through. Slowly he remembered being caught in a whirlwind. When had it happened? The nurse patted him on the shoulder and prepared him for the operation. He whetted a razor on a leather belt and daubed some gauze in chloroform.

The airman looked at him. The sound of an engine came to his mind. Was he travelling on an aeroplane when the accident happened? It was impossible to remember what that aeroplane looked like or whether he had been a passenger or its pilot. He was still trying to make sense when the nurse pressed the gauze with the chloroform on his face. A saccharine taste burned his throat, and he began to faint. The nurse lathered his head before taking the sharpened razor. After he had shaved a patch of hair, he lifted the pilot from the cot and put him on a stretcher. He was ready to leave for the operating room when the medic walked in.

'Are we ready?' he asked. He leaned over the stretcher. 'We have to relieve intracerebral pressure, lieutenant,' he said. 'Just a little bleeding between your encephalon and your cranium. Nothing to worry about.'

Air Lieutenant Kimon slowly shut his eyes against his will.

The moon rose silently. Inside his tent Major Porfirio yawned, moved the flap aside and looked out. Lit by the moon, the camp seemed no more real than the props on a theatrical stage. Clouds appeared over the hills. Moments later a wind started that made the camp resound with noise: unlatched lorry doors banged, tarpaulins flapped, the Christian cross on the end of the flagpole spun like a weathercock. Major Porfirio pulled his head inside, sat at his desk and poured himself a glass of cordial. It was the only drink left apart from warm water and bad coffee.

He was young for a major and even more so for a Chief of Staff. A bayonet slash across his face gave him an austere expression. There was also a deeper, hidden cut: he thought the war purposeless. But he was a soldier and had complied. He refilled his glass. The brown dust that covered him from head to toe made him seem like a figure out of an old photograph. He drank and had another look outside, where three tattered flags hung from the pole in the middle of the camp. Two were the flags of the infantry regiments and were embroidered with the Virgin and the names of the victorious battles of the Balkan wars: it had been a mission he had also taken part in but, unlike this war, he was proud of it. The third and smallest flag, with Saint George slaying the dragon, belonged to the cavalry regiment. Satisfied no one was near, Major Porfirio returned to his desk and took the cover off his typewriter.

He had only managed a sentence when the sound of

footsteps interrupted him. He removed the paper from the cylinder, hid it under his tunic and gave permission to enter. The corporal walked in and saluted.

'All quiet,' he reported.

Major Porfirio relaxed.

'It's you. Up at this hour?'

The corporal removed his cap and used it to brush the dust off his clothes. His shirt was missing some buttons. He held his carbine and his pockets sagged with bullets. His half-empty cartridge belt crossed his chest: Major Porfirio called to mind the whipping of the horse.

'I'm on patrol,' the corporal said.

'Good. Then we'll do it tonight.'

The corporal sat down. He kept his eyes fixed on the entrance, listening. He started tapping his foot. After a while he said, 'If this weather continues, there will be no dust left in this place by dawn.'

His superior rocked back and forth in his chair, listening calmly to the wind. Lying in their cots and wrapped in their coats, his men could do nothing but wait. His first and utmost responsibility was towards them. All his efforts were to enlighten and inspire them – and keep them alive, of course. But the corporal was his only convert. He shook his head.

'We'll still be here,' he said.

The corporal did not understand.

'Comrade?'

'There'll be no dust in the morning but we'll still be here.'

The wind blew.

'One fellow-traveller out of a thousand men,' the major said. 'Some achievement.'

The corporal shrugged.

'You tried your best, comrade.'

'A waste of time. The handbills are fodder for the mules and kindling for the padre's brazier.'

The corporal chuckled, 'Ha ha.' His superior shot him an annoyed glance.

'What's so funny?'

The corporal looked away, next to the typewriter. A storm lamp on the desk gave the two faces an amber tint. A few mosquitoes had discovered the source of light. Life operated by a hierarchy of size, quantity or strength: the insect, the lizard, the beast. In the scale of the universe, the man was still of infinitesimal importance. The corporal searched his pockets and found the medal he had received in the first year of the war. For a while he fiddled with it.

'So, I have to give this back?'

'All decorations should be returned as a protest against the imperialist policies that led to the war.'

Major Porfirio remembered one of his comrade's recent enquiries and took out a pamphlet from his pocket.

'This will answer your questions regarding the concept of surplus value.'

The corporal put the pamphlet and the medal in his pocket and blew out his cheeks. The storm was not going to wane soon. Dust crept into the tent from underneath the tarpaulin. A passing sense of menace came over the cavalryman but then he realised the weather was his ally: no one would be out that night.

'We should've gone when we had the chance, major. The comrades at the railway would've helped us.'

'You could have, corporal. I don't agree with the Party on this one. As long as the brigade exists I can't abandon it.'

It was getting cold in the tent. The corporal hugged himself and glanced round with boredom. He saw the major gazing at the storm lantern, and it suddenly crossed his mind how different they were for fellow conspirators.

He said, 'I have to continue my rounds.'

Their embrace was both affectionate and ceremonial.

'Come back in an hour,' Major Porfirio said. 'I should have everything ready.'

When he was alone again, he sat with his back to the lamp. His coat dangling from a pole felt like a reminder of the fate that awaited him if he were ever arrested. He had to print the handbills. He took out the sheet he had hidden under his tunic and fed it into his typewriter again. A mimeograph was in a crate, and when he finished typing, he put the machine on his desk. He mounted the typed sheet on the cylinder and fed paper squares through it. There was something defeated in the way he turned the handle, humming at the same time the Internationale.

Air Lieutenant Kimon awoke from his sleep in the dark and tasted the chloroform in his mouth. He spat several times on the floor and studied his surroundings. A few oil lamps across the tent threw their light on the other wounded. He could not see clearly. The concussion was almost gone, but the anaesthetic had left a mist over his eyes that was slow to dissolve and gave his surroundings a haunted quality. This was his first encounter with the consequences of war. He was always based hundreds of miles behind the front line, in airfields set up on requisitioned farms and country estates. He had witnessed several battles but only from the air.

He raised his hand to his head and felt the square patch of shaved hair. In its middle he discovered the metal disc that plugged the perforation of the trephine. He shivered. Around him the other patients snored. The proximity of other people made him uncomfortable. He had been an only child, sheltered from the world in his formative years by private tuition. His fastidiousness had persisted at the Swiss boarding-school and the University of Vienna, where he had always had private accommodation. He left his bed, found his clothes and dressed quietly. Outside, he was pleased to feel the wind against his face but not over the tender patch on his head. He quickly put on his leather helmet and fastened the strap. The mounting storm swept across the camp, carrying away pieces of tarpaulin, cups and pots, the ashes of the campfires.

He had the idea of sharing a cigarette with the sentries. He expected there would be guards at the corral, but when he came to it, he saw there was none: they had probably taken shelter, waiting for the weather to clear. Behind the fence the dromedaries sat quietly on the ground, ruminating, oblivious to the wind. It was different for the other animals. The mules and horses brayed and neighed, choked on the dust, tried to free their legs from the hobbles.

He took out his cigarette case, but the wind snatched it from his hands. He went down on his knees and felt about in the dark. He was still searching for the repoussé case when he saw, among the legs of the horses, an officer. He did not stand up. He observed the officer moving about as if he were searching for something. Finally the officer stopped. In the moonlight Air Lieutenant Kimon saw him remove the blindfold from a horse with a scarred back, and then the hobbles from its legs. The officer had only a moment to pat the horse before the animal understood it was free. It cleared the fence with an easy jump and disappeared into the night. Having watched the animal's flight, the officer left the corral quietly.

Only then did Air Lieutenant Kimon stand up. He had made no effort to stop the officer. From the first moment he saw him in the moonlight he had recognised him but was so intrigued he had decided not to raise the alarm. He found his platinum case and lit a cigarette, shoved his hands in his pockets and set off again on his walk, thinking of what he had witnessed. The storm waned, and the dust began to settle on the lorries, the tents, the artillery guns. The mast with the regimental flags in the middle of the camp leaned to one side. The soldiers emerged from the tents and set about digging out the lorries buried in the dirt. But it was futile. Soon the storm was heard approaching again. They secured everything they could, tied the lorry doors and tarpaulins with rope, covered the gun muzzles, took down the flags. Then the wind arrived, but this time the whirlwind did not just bring dust to the camp but what seemed from afar to be a flock of seagulls. In fact they were handbills. Apart from the usual proclamations that the war was an imperialist undertaking and the government was entirely responsible for the mess they were in, this time the handbills also included a denunciation of the recent thefts, calling them the act of a counter-revolutionary traitor.

6

It was the first night in many weeks that Brigadier Nestor, surrendering to homesickness, did not sleep in his uniform. On nights like these, he had the habit of wearing the loose white nightshirt with flared sleeves and wooden buttons down the front that his wife had packed in his trunk in order to remind him of their bed. He had laughed at her suggestion then, but three years had passed since he had left home, and the nightshirt never failed to work its magic on him.

His wife had taken its secret to her grave. She had boiled the fabric in a stew of herbs, where she had also added several pellets of ambergris, the secretion of a spermaceti whale caught in the Tropics. It was this last ingredient that made the brigadier feel a little like the prophet Jonah whenever he dressed in the nightshirt before its rare perfume sent him to sleep and unlocked his memory.

But on cold nights like this, wearing the nightshirt did not help his rheumatism. Brigadier Nestor felt uncomfortable. He stood up and searched in his trunk for his nightcap. Despite wearing his coat over his nightshirt, the cold still gripped his chest like a vice. With the cap pulled down over his forehead and ears, he returned to his cot, blew out the lamp and buried himself under the blankets. The wind continued to perforate the tent – an old tarpaulin stretched over a framework made of two poles and a few lengths of rope. Brigadier Nestor tried to shelter from the cold like a soldier caught in crossfire.

When the storm slowed down, he managed to fall asleep. He was soon dreaming.

At first he dreamed he was back home and the war was over. He had been demobilised with the rank of lieutenant-general and lived quietly in the capital on a good pension. For a while he enjoyed the peace he could not afford while awake. But it disappeared suddenly, and he found himself in that town again: he was dreaming about the massacre.

It was a town of single-storey houses round a small square. It was raining, and the houses were sinking into the mud. There was a ring of soldiers in the earthen square, while in the middle, herded together, were the villagers. The soldiers wore their coats and helmets, but the people stood knee deep in the mud, half-naked, drenched and silent. Brigadier Nestor twitched in his cot and his breathing became heavier. In his dream the soldiers fitted the bayonets on their rifles and the rain gathered strength. The brigadier knew what would happen next: an order was going to be given. He shuddered from fear as he struggled to prevent in his nightmare something that in reality had already happened. His dream took its usual course.

Some time later – he did not know how long – he awoke with his face in a puddle of sweat. Since the collapse of the front, he had seen many ditches overflowing with bodies, but they were mostly military casualties. For these dead from either side he felt nothing any more – apart perhaps from a certain curiosity regarding the manner of their death. They appeared no more human to him than the mummies in an archaeological museum. But the memory of the town was different. Those had been civilians, and it was he who had ordered their execution. He had searched long before he had discovered his only source of solace: it was time for his morphia shot.

The dawn found him at his desk, shaven and dressed in his breeches, vest and boots. With the pair of compasses, ruler and pencil in hand, he was leaning over the maps. His night torment had left its dark circles round his eyes. Someone asked permission to enter.

Major Porfirio walked in and saluted. He had shaved, leaving a trimmed moustache that turned upwards at the tips. The brigadier studied the groomed moustache, the skin that was tanned by the sun, the dark eyes: it could well be the face of the enemy. He nodded at his Chief of Staff.

'Good, Porfirio. That beard was too thick. I could hardly hear what you were saying.'

Where his breeches ended, a pair of scrawny legs extended downwards and disappeared into his unlaced boots. Without socks or leather leggings, the major's feet seemed ridiculously small. Brigadier Nestor felt he was a grotesque character in a fairy tale for children.

'Thank you for indulging the fancies of an old goblin,' he said.

Major Porfirio removed his sola topi and sat on the edge of the brigadier's cot. He noticed the signs of a tormented sleep: the blankets were in a jumble, there were sweat marks on the pillow, a nightcap was on the floor. The brigadier began to change into a clean uniform.

'What month is it?' the old man asked.

'September.'

'Of course. It's as if my bones are being crushed with pestle and mortar.'

He had suffered from rheumatism for years, but the privations of the long march had caused his condition to deteriorate. He folded his nightshirt and stored it in the trunk with a silent promise never to wear it again unless he was lying in his bed at home. He slung the braces of his breeches over his shoulders, sat in his chair and started rubbing his knees. Then he bent down to tie his laces, an undertaking that was as sentimental as an act of penance.

'I'm turning into a fossil,' he said.

It was as if he had aged overnight. The major opened his mouth to say something, but his superior started first.

'It's a direct challenge to my authority. Everyone knows how much I like cigars.'

'A horse also went missing during the storm,' the major said.

But his commanding officer paid no attention. He twisted the tip of his moustache.

'My list of suspects is longer than the catalogue of the library of Alexandria, but I'll pare it down. The only things aplenty in this place are dust and time.'

The rage pressed against his chest. After the violence of the previous night, a pleasant wind shook the tent and brought the old man back to reality.

'Mm? Yes, the storm. I understand it caused problems?'

His Chief of Staff had already compiled a list of the damage to the materiel. The brigadier gave it a look but did not let his subordinate read it to him. He started to rap his fingers on his desk without speaking. After a while he stood up.

'I heard a story once,' he said. 'On some island or other, a seasonal wind exists that can drive one insane. When it blows, everyone take to their houses. The instant madness of those caught in the open causes them to hang themselves, throw themselves off a cliff or drown themselves in the wells.' He clasped his hands behind his back and walked round his desk. 'That's what I was told. Of course it could all just be a myth invented by the islanders to cover up the punishment of molesters, adulterers and sheep stealers.' He took a deep breath. 'But no matter how evil that wind is, no one has ever reported it carrying away a grown horse. Or putting Bolshevik ideas into people's heads.'

Feeling his strength drain away quickly, he sat in his chair again. He was having a bad headache. Flies flew in through the entrance of the tent. The wind had stopped, and the heat grew. He wiped his forehead with his cuff.

'Dissemination of anti-national literature in wartime is high treason and, therefore, punishable by death.' He took a handbill from his pocket and looked at it. 'The Red Scourge,' he said. 'So, it thrives in this climate, too. I thought the bloodbath of our retreat would've satisfied the traitor. The hatred of whoever writes these is unquenchable.'

He crumpled up the piece of paper into a ball and tossed it away. He sat back and crossed his hands over his belly.

'More and more this adventure reminds me of *The Odyssey*,' he said.

Outside a soldier with his rifle slung over his shoulder paced up and down. Walking back and forth, he was like the statue in a bell tower set in motion by its clock. It was an image of peace: the chiming of the bells in a town somewhere in Switzerland or the Netherlands, places the devastation of war would perhaps never reach. Someone entered the tent.

'This is the soldier whose horse has disappeared,' Major Porfirio said.

The corporal stood to attention and saluted. His uniform hung on him like clothes on a scarecrow. He lowered his hand and waited. Brigadier Nestor waved him at ease.

He asked, 'Did you witness the incident?'

'No, my brigadier.'

'Any witnesses come forward?'

The major replied that there had been none. Brigadier Nestor could still not forget the Bolshevik conspiracy.

'Do you know anything about the other incident last night?' he asked the corporal.

'Sir?'

'The handbills.'

The non-commissioned officer gave a negative answer. Brigadier Nestor pursed his lips.

'It was a bad storm, my brigadier,' the corporal said. 'We had to take shelter.'

'A storm?' Brigadier Nestor asked. 'Yes, the storm. Of course. You took shelter.'

He needed morphia. In the roll call that morning, no one was missing: whoever set the horse loose had stayed behind.

'There's only one explanation,' he said. 'Sabotage by the Bolsheviks. Thank you, corporal. You too, major. Both dismissed.'

The corporal saluted and left. He wandered about the camp until he came to the fence of the corral, where he leaned against the wire. He did not expect the disappearance of the gelding to affect him. It was not merely the fact that he was on foot now – he felt lonely too. It was his loneliness that had led him to join the Party.

It had started with an advertisement he had placed in the personal column of a national newspaper back home, asking to correspond with young women. He had written: *Decorated hero* . . . even though at that time he had only seen the front line through his binoculars. By the time his only reply arrived from a woman in Salonika, he had received his first medal and been promoted to the rank of corporal.

They wrote to each other frequently, but no matter how many times he asked her, she never sent him her picture. He himself had sent her a photograph of himself, coloured by hand and mounted on cardboard. It showed him in parade uniform in front of an Oriental landscape, cap under his arm, elbow resting on a pillar. After a few letters, she had mentioned the political situation. It was a topic the corporal had found uninteresting at first. But as his affection for his correspondent grew, he started not only to agree with her but also to add to her radical views in order to please her. Then, in her ninth letter, she had revealed Major Porfirio's name: he was the commissar secretly in charge of indoctrinating the brigade.

Standing at the fence of the corral, the corporal watched a soldier brushing the animals. The breeze wafted their reek across to him. There was something of the homeland about it. Suddenly a thought crossed his mind: he must go to Salonika and find his correspondent. She loved him and would not deny him. But would he make it out of this place alive? It was the flight of his horse that gave him the idea. It would be difficult to find his way alone, but one man could travel faster than a whole brigade, with its artillery guns and the wounded and the lorries breaking down every few hours. One man could also slip easily through enemy lines. The brigade would have to engage, and many would die, of course.

He felt the excitement of his decision. He had to plot this well. It was desertion: if caught he could expect the firing squad. But nothing could wipe the smile off his face. When he walked away from the corral, he had already begun to plan his escape.

The storm had set the sky spinning in circles. All day, drawn into the centre of the whirlpool, clouds had gathered, and by late afternoon they had filled the sky. Behind the leaden, low-hovering clouds the sun glimmered like a distant lighthouse. The air was humid. In the evening the first drops fell. Soon the rain grew into a storm that melted the dry earth. For several hours the soldiers struggled to save lorries and artillery guns before the mud swallowed up the materiel. Only when the equipment stood again on firm ground were the troops allowed to rest under the incessant rain. Autumn had arrived: travelling would be more difficult from now on.

Standing in front of the stove, the cook was crying. He looked above his head where the canvas canopy had begun to sag from the rain. The ropes stretched, and the poles creaked. Wondering how long it would be before something snapped, he continued to peel onions. He threw the chopped onion into the frying pan, wiped his tears on his apron and started to hum. While the onion sautéed, he removed the layer of mould from a corned beef tin and added its contents to the pan.

The rain poured from the edges of the canopy, and thunder cracked. Stirring the meat he remembered life before his conscription. He used to work in the kitchen of an old steamship that twice a week did the round trip from Piraeus to the islands, and he swore that once he had glimpsed a mermaid surfacing on the bow.

Caleb came with the padre. Father Simeon studied the sagging canvas roof.

'What are you going to do about this?' he asked.

The cook assessed the growing problem above his head. 'Nothing.'

'It can't support the weight for much longer.'

'I'll look at it as soon as I've had my meal.'

Caleb sat on his hind legs and fixed his eyes on the cook.

'Maybe something for the dog?' the padre asked.

The cook gave the padre the corned beef tin. A burst of rain fell on the stove, and the sizzling startled the dog. There was still a little meat left in the tin.

'There are maggots in this,' Father Simeon said.

'Then you have to give it back. The medic pays a dozen cigarettes per can of worms.'

'The medic?'

'They eat the germs in the wounds. He economises on carbolic.'

Father Simeon looked at the maggots. He thought, the world abounds with small daily miracles.

'The spontaneous birth of worms in rotting matter is a phenomenon godless Darwin never managed to explain,' he said.

The cook took the tin from his hands and put it in a safe place. He served himself half the fried beef and ate standing up. Next to him Father Simeon could not stop thinking about the maggots. The rain soon put out the fire in the stove. The two men and the animal squeezed round the stove that was already cooling down. Holding the mess tin at his chin, the cook ate with his fingers.

'Provisions are running out, Father. Soon you'll have to show me how Christ fed the five thousand with seven loaves.'

'It was five loaves and two fish,' the padre said. 'But you're right to be confused. Elsewhere in the Bible Matthew says the Lord fed in fact seven thousand with seven loaves and a few fish. In any case miracles only happen in exceptional circumstances. I suggest you take the Holy Sacrament and pray. And not just for your own good but for the salvation of the whole brigade.'

The rain came down heavily, hitting the roof like lead shot. The dog curled up at Father Simeon's feet.

'Once it rained fish in a neighbouring parish,' the padre continued. 'If I hadn't seen it with my own eyes I wouldn't have believed it.'

'What sort of fish?'

'Whitebait. The human mind can't begin to comprehend God's ways.'

The cook served himself the rest of the food. Father Simeon studied him.

'Do you ever wake up at night?' he asked.

A shadow passed over the other man's face: he knew the padre was referring to the massacre. The truth was that the ghosts had also been appearing to him.

'I generally sleep well.'

'And the memory of the events don't bother you?'

'I'm only here to cook, Father. The only authority I am invested with is what to serve tomorrow.' He spat out a piece of bone. 'All other decisions I leave to my superiors.'

The tarpaulin above their heads creaked under the weight of the rain.

'I envy you. *My* superior lets me make all the decisions myself.'

'I see. The bishop?'

'The Lord.'

The cook stretched his neck out of the canopy and drank

from the pouring rain. The wind travelled between the camp and the hills, bringing back sand, dust and gravel and mixing them with the rain. Under the canvas roof, the two men could only wait. The padre took out a bundle of paper: the Genesis and Exodus pages which Caleb had torn from his bible. He searched through the loose pages and cleared his throat.

'And God said unto Noah, the end of all flesh is come before me. For the earth is filled with violence through them. And, behold, I will destroy them with the earth.'

He had no time to read more. A loud crack interrupted him. He had only just turned his head and noticed the snapping pole when the canopy began to rip from its edge. Then it burst open and let loose a torrent of water, which fell over the two men and the dog and threw them instantly face down into the mud.

7

When will this torment end? Major Porfirio stood in front of the mirror. The narrowed eyebrows, the furrow in the bridge of the nose, the stubborn lip: like most men of authority, he had sculpted that face by himself. He pulled the braces off his shoulders and his trousers dropped to his ankles. He felt tired and disheartened. He had to admit that his propaganda mission had failed. There was not much point in continuing with it; he only risked being caught. The sound of rain against the tarpaulin gave him some sort of comfort. He raised the wick in the lamp and looked closer in the mirror. The shadows of his cheekbones, the stubble on his chin, his long moustache fitted the portrait of a beaten man.

His underwear was a tattered undershirt and a pair of long johns. He removed his undershirt. The sun had baked his face and neck, but the rest of his skin was soft and white, save for some patches of hard-crusted dirt: more the body of a peasant than a warrior. They had not fired a shot in weeks – just marched in circles. Throughout the war the major had maintained his opposition to the campaign without doubting his convictions, but in battle he would throw himself at the enemy. He found a stiff brush. From the pole of his tent hung a cavalry tunic, a sword with tassels, a rimmed helmet dented by shrapnel. His riding uniform reminded him of his horse. She had bled to death in the first week of the withdrawal from a bullet she had taken in the neck. Rubbing his back with the brush, he thought about the animal. Now he was riding a postman's motorcycle.

From not far away came the noise of ripping canvas and snapping wood – probably a roof, collapsing from the weight of the rain. He thought he heard the padre's voice and a sudden cry from his dog but paid no more attention. Under his desk were his riding boots and next to them a crate with second-hand books: *Socialism: Utopian and Scientific, Critique of Political Economy, Imperialism: the Highest Stage of Capitalism* . . . There were several others. Major Porfirio picked one up and thumbed the pages. He had trouble understanding them but knew in his heart of hearts that they were right. He would have to be deaf and blind not to notice the unfairness of the world: reaction to injustice was an instinct. He put the book back and chose another. He had to search through two more before discovering the velvet pouch. He spread it open on his desk.

It contained his medals from the Balkan wars. He had been a second lieutenant fresh from the Academy when he had been sent to Macedonia, where he had been quickly promoted to captain. Painted by a patriotic itinerant painter, his badly drawn portrait still decorated the walls of coffee shops in villages liberated by the company under his command: a man in an ancient helmet and body armour, shield and javelin, with a pistol round his waist.

He arranged the medals on his desk like jewellery, starting with his favourites: a silver cross on a ribbon with blue-and-white stripes, and a bronze cross with crossed swords on the end of a red-and-blue ribbon. One had been awarded to him when the War Minister had heard of the young officer at the front who had thrown himself on top of a live grenade that had rolled into the pit where he and several of his men had taken cover. The grenade had turned out to be a tortoise blown into the pit by the explosion of an artillery shell, but that did not stop the minister from pinning some days later the Silver Medal for Valour on the brave officer's chest. The other decoration, the War Cross Third Class, he had received after capturing a submerged Ottoman general hiding in a flooded marsh with a reed in his mouth.

Recollecting these and other adventures, while still rubbing his back with the brush, Major Porfirio could suppress neither his pride nor his sadness. He would have to return all his medals when the expedition was over and resign from the army for the sake of politics. It had been a difficult decision, but these were exciting times Europe was living through, what with the founding of the soviets . . . He had done his duty even though he disagreed with the campaign. It was his responsibility towards his men that made him remain at his post. Yet now the war had been lost, and, while the generals were back home, he was still here.

He thought about the only soldier he had managed to convert to communism and chuckled bitterly. The idea that the Party should reply to soldiers' advertisements in the personal columns of the national press had been his. How would the corporal react if he knew that his correspondent was not the young woman of his dreams but an overweight and bearded commissar in Salonika?

He put on his coat, took down his helmet, removed the glass cover from the storm lantern and held the helmet over the flame. When it was so hot he could hold it no more, he hid it under the blanket. Waiting for his cot to warm up, he sat at his desk and took from the crate a book entitled *Origin of the Family, Private Property and the State*. Pencil in hand, it was not long before his head came to rest on the well-thumbed pages, and he began to snore with a whistling noise.

Moments after the canopy had caved in, a squad of drenched *evzones* wearing short tunics and ammunition belts across the chest passed near the field kitchen. Unaware of the disaster, they would have carried on had they not heard the yapping of the dog. When they realised what had happened, they stacked their rifles and rushed to save the men.

First they dug up the cook and sat him on the ground. He had to take deep breaths and spit out a lot of mud before he could speak.

'The padre,' he said.

Caleb was already digging into the mud furiously. The weight of the flooded canopy had toppled the stove, and the padre lay under it. The soldiers managed to lift the cast-iron stove and pull him out. He was shaken. The first thing he did was to feel his pockets.

'My Bible! Find my Bible!'

Covered in mud, his face seemed like a clay mask. Behind it his left eye moved from side to side. He shook off his helpers and began to move in circles, uttering loud croaks. The soldiers stepped back and watched. The padre continued to move in circles with his head bent and then suddenly fell to his knees and turned silent. At his feet was a small heap of pulp. As soon as Father Simeon took it in his hands, it broke to pieces.

'Ruined,' he mumbled. 'Now we're *truly* lost.'

He meant what he said. He always considered the Book to be one's only map in the journey towards salvation. He looked at its remains with despair. He would have been less devastated had the brigadier's maps met a similar fate. He stood up, wavering. The soldiers held him by his arms.

'The Lord shall never allow unrepentant souls out of Hell,' he said.

The rain fell from clouds that were dark and heavy like smoke. The padre observed the wet faces round him, with an eye that was full of pity.

'I'm surrounded by dead men,' he said, trembling with fear.

The cook washed the mud from the padre's face until the beard, the ploughed forehead, the cracked lips had regained some of their life.

'Take him to the infirmary,' he said.

'Leave me alone,' the padre hissed. 'I have to go to church. I need to pray for your souls.'

The *evzones* took a step back – there was still some authority left in Father Simeon's voice. He picked up his cap, wrung the water out and began to walk towards his tent. The dog followed close behind.

He did not appear at the next roll call, nor was he seen anywhere in the camp all day. Only those who happened to walk past his church of the Cappadocian Fathers heard his voice: a weak and suppliant whimper that was a far cry from the usual vociferations of his sermons.

News of the accident spread fast. After evening mess the major was asked to report to brigade command. Brigadier Nestor was sitting at his desk when his Chief of Staff entered, making cigars from a bundle of tobacco leaves. Immersed in his task, he did not notice his subordinate until some time later, when he raised his head and saw the silhouette in the dark. Major Porfirio stood to attention. The old officer did not return his salute.

'Come closer, major.'

There was a crude cigar press on his desk. Brigadier Nestor wrapped several leaves together and tried to roll them, but they were too dry, and they cracked in his fingers. He bit his lip and started again. Every time he had to use his hands to perform some delicate job his rheumatism made it feel as if he were wearing gloves. It took him several failed attempts before he gave up. He took out a pipe and filled it with the tobacco scattered on his desk. He sat back in his chair and smoked, relighting his pipe now and then. He seemed to have forgotten the major. His maps were on the floor under the table. His private letters were mixed up with his blankets. Major Porfirio glanced at the mess.

'I don't see much future in cigarettes,' the brigadier said.

'They're nothing but paper, hay and a pinch of the cheapest tobacco in the middle. A pipe is much better.' He puffed out a cloud of smoke. 'So. The padre went insane. An interesting development.' He chuckled. 'He brainwashed himself by reading the Bible night and day, eh?'

'His Bible was all but ruined by the rain,' Major Porfirio said.

'Thank God. Peace and quiet at last. His megaphone was worse than the Furies.' The brigadier lifted the cover of the lamp and lit his pipe again. 'I always thought his attitude was detrimental to troop morale.' He picked up a map from the floor and tore off a large piece, in which he wrapped the tobacco leaves. 'I shall carry this tobacco with me at all times. It's the only way of making sure that no one steals it.'

The major looked at the torn map with a frown. His commanding officer waved his hand in a sign of indifference.

'Don't worry about these, Porfirio. They are worse than Columbus's maps. You may go.'

It was a night of clear skies and dim stars. Two days earlier it had been a bright, full moon, but now the crescent was sallow and grim. Major Porfirio felt suffocated. His mission of enlightenment kept him busy during the long days of the retreat and helped him preserve his sanity. Now that this task had failed, he wished he were home. He looked to the sky. He made out the North Star and raised his head to the left to find the constellation of Lyra. Vega, its brightest star, seemed that night no more brilliant than a firefly. It was as if a paper screen stood between Heaven and earth. When he lowered his head, he was surprised to see the soldiers still sitting round the campfires. He lit a match, checked his watch and pursed his lips: the bugler should have called lights out half an hour ago. After a brief search he found him sitting under the flag, talking to the airman. Immediately he saw his superior, the bugler sprang to his feet, put the bugle under his arm and saluted.

76

'My major. I was about to commence.'

The brass coating had rubbed off the bugle, and its gold-threaded cord had lost its tassel. In its bell was the dent from the time the bugler had brought the instrument down on the head of a brigand. Major Porfirio waved him at ease.

'We were discussing my demobilisation, my major,' the bugler said. 'The lieutenant is kind enough to promise to help me find a job in a cabaret when all this is over.'

He raised the bugle but was so nervous that he blew off key.

'Lights out if you please, bugler,' the major said without anger. 'Not a foxtrot.'

Before the call had ended, the fires were disappearing, and the camp faded from the plain. Air Lieutenant Kimon took out his case and offered the major a cigarette. It was an ill-omened event that started innocently, like the eating of the forbidden fruit or a child at play with a box of matches. The army officer studied it. The moonlight was reflecting upon his face from the platinum case. The airman soon noticed his indignation but guessed the wrong reason for it.

'No, these aren't rationed,' he said. 'They are the best Turkish. Go ahead, major.'

But it was the expensive case that Major Porfirio was looking at with such contempt.

'I've seen whole families killed for less,' he said.

The lieutenant knitted his eyebrows and nodded.

'Yes, we heard such stories at the squadron.'

The major looked at the night sky.

'War must be a lesser affair from up there,' he said.

'Lesser?'

'One doesn't witness the horror.'

'I almost died trying to find you, major.'

'A blind man would've done a better job.' Major Porfirio lowered his eyes to the cigarette case. 'Don't wave this around, lieutenant. There has been a series of thefts.'

The airman smiled.

'Couldn't I at least trust an officer?'

The major's dark eyes, black hair and olive skin were the opposite of the younger airman's Teutonic beauty.

'Even officers are sometimes human, lieutenant,' he said.

'My experience shows otherwise,' the airman joked.

His impertinence increased Major Porfirio's anger. Until that moment his contempt for the aristocracy had been little more than a theoretical abstraction: the bourgeoisie, the government, the foreign imperialist powers. Now it had found a face. The great revolutionary leaders had for some time been the object of his affections – but a doctrine needs both its gods and its demons.

'Report to the medical officer in the morning and volunteer your services,' the major ordered. 'Let's hope you're better at emptying bedpans than flying a plane.'

Air Lieutenant Kimon's aversion to authority stemmed from his childhood. His father was an autocrat who had forced him to bathe in icy cold water because he believed that it was beneficial to a man's constitution, he had banned the reading of modern poetry because it nurtured the danger of melancholy, and as for the solitary sin of onanism, which he had once caught his son committing, he had shipped all the way from England a patented contraption that restrained its user so that he would not turn overnight into a blind idiot.

Air Lieutenant Kimon stood to attention and saluted his superior.

'As you wish, major.'

When the two officers walked away in opposite directions, the major had made an implacable enemy.

Father Simeon unscrewed the bottom of the lamp and added a few drops of oil. Above his head ran lines of string where the damp yellowed pages of his bible hung down, held with clothes pegs. He put on his glasses and examined the pages closely. Under the ink blotches, most of the text was fortunately visible. He pulled down a few pages and hung the lamp round his neck. As soon as he found his megaphone, he made the sign of the cross and left the tent.

Not far away, covered with the blanket, the brigadier was dreaming he was on board a train travelling through olive groves on a cloudless day. Sitting alone in a private compartment with leather seats, he was smoking a big cigar. With his thick book in hand, he was lost in the Greek and Roman myths. On the table in front of him, a glass filled with absinthe chimed to the vibrations of the car. Suddenly a distant voice intruded upon his happy journey like a conductor's announcement:

'*Yet thou shalt be brought down to hell, to the sides of the pit. They that see thee shall narrowly look upon thee, and consider thee, saying, Is this the man that made the earth to tremble, that did shake kingdoms; that made the world as a wilderness, and destroyed the cities thereof; that opened not the house of his prisoners?*'

The brigadier raised his head from his pillow and rubbed his eyes. It took him some time to become aware that he was indeed awake. Holding his breath he listened.

'*But thou art cast out of thy grave like an abominable branch, and as the raiment of those that are slain, thrust through with a sword, that go down to the stones of the pit; as a carcase trodden under feet.*'

'In the name of mercy,' he said when he realised who the voice belonged to. The invisible narrator continued gravely and monotonously.

'*Thou shalt not be joined with them in burial, because thou hast destroyed thy land, and slain thy people . . .*'

When the padre moved on and there was silence again, Brigadier Nestor was left shivering. His feet jutted out from his campaign cot. He imagined himself strapped on to

Procrustes' bed. He had still not fallen asleep when somewhere across the camp another headache was already brewing for him: also lying on his back, with his hands folded under his head and his eyes open, the corporal was planning his escape for the night of the next new moon.

Part 2

The Town

8

The *hamam* was located in a quiet street behind the market.
It was an ochre building with a dome of peeling plaster and
the façade of a country chapel. Immediately past its entrance
was a square court with cubicles round a stone fountain, each
with a bench and a row of shelves. The baths themselves were
a large steamy chamber whose floor was decorated with
geometric mosaics. An archway of thin columns ran round
the room, where the coal furnaces used for heating were.
In the middle of the chamber, lit by shafts of daylight through
the windows of the dome, was a marble platform. On it at
that moment, prone and naked, lay a big man.

The schoolmaster dipped the ladle in the pail and sprinkled
the coals with slow, stupefied movements. Hot vapours and
the smell of essential oils rose from the grate and covered his
body. He closed his eyes and folded his hands over his belly.
Motionless and prostrate under layers of steam, he gave the
appearance of a corpse wrapped in a shroud. Some time later
the creak of the door awakened him. The schoolmaster
squinted at the shadow moving behind the steam.

'Is that you, Yusuf?'

'At your service,' replied a cheerful voice.

The young attendant approached the platform with effort.
Deformed by a teenage attack of tuberculosis, his back had a
large hump. On his dark Arab face his eyes shone with a
combination of brightness and humility. He put down the
pail and smiled. His teeth were as bright as the whites of his

eyes. The pail contained a large towel, a bowl with a handle, a bar of soap and a brush.

'Isn't Mr Othon asleep?'

The schoolmaster closed his eyes and waved to him to proceed. The attendant rolled up his sleeves, filled the pail with hot water and started rubbing the other man's back. Above the columns and across all four walls, a painted frieze showed a floral scene of acanthus leaves and branches of pomegranates among images of lovemaking. After washing out the suds with tepid water, the Arab massaged his customer's skin for a long time and then filled the pail with cold water and splashed it over him. The schoolmaster squealed.

'Damn you, Yusuf,' he said. 'Did you bring that water all the way from Antarctica?'

He jumped off the platform and wrapped himself in the towel. When his teeth stopped chattering, he asked for his clothes. The attendant shuffled his slippers towards the door.

'In my cubicle you will also find my bag,' the schoolmaster said. 'Bring it to the garden.'

The man nodded.

'Does Mr Othon want his *narghile*?'

The schoolmaster smacked his lips.

'An excellent idea, Yusuf.'

He made his way to the garden, whistling. As soon as he stepped into the courtyard, the weather boosted his joy. It was a sunny afternoon with a mellow and golden light: autumn had finally arrived. The garden was surrounded on all four sides with plastered walls the colour of peach, where stray ivies had grown over the years. In the honeycomb holes at the top of the walls, pigeons had made their nests. There were hibiscus shrubs in the garden and a narrow juniper heavy with berries, whose shadow fell over a pond full of algae and goldfish. In the green water, the fish swam slowly, never touching each other. The schoolmaster carried a chair to the shadow of the wall.

In a moment Yusuf came with his clothes, a leather brief-case and the *narghile*. They were the clothes of a bachelor: the worn shirt collar, the extra piece of fabric sewn on the seat of the trousers, a bent paperclip in place of the missing button on the jacket. Humming, the schoolmaster dressed with the help of the Arab.

'They don't make suits like this any more, Yusuf,' he said. 'I had it sewn when I was promoted to schoolmaster.'

The attendant looked at the shabby old-fashioned suit and nodded approvingly.

'It's very good,' he said.

Mr Othon's hand searched for the collar button but it, too, had fallen victim to the anarchy that ruled his life; it had fallen off earlier when he had undressed in the *camekan* before entering the baths. He tightened his tie over his loose collar and asked for his jacket. Yusuf held it up for him.

'This fabric is not only exquisite,' Mr Othon said and pushed his arms into the sleeves, 'but also impenetrable. It has survived fourteen years of student bombardment.'

'Is that right?' Yusuf asked appreciatively. 'It seems like you bought it yesterday.'

His customer put on his white felt hat and checked the time on a sundial among the hibiscus. He sat down in the shade and opened his briefcase. Tied with an elastic band was a bundle of answer sheets to the problems he had set the previous day on the laws of gravity. He put on his glasses and had only had a quick look through before knitting his brows and making reproving sounds.

'Cretins,' he said. 'They made a preserve out of Newton's apples.' He sucked the tube of the *narghile*. 'Look at this, my friend. And they're descendants of Heraclitus.'

Yusuf did not understand but acknowledged the comment with a grunt. Unlike his customer he himself was dressed with less consequence but more prudence for such a warm afternoon: a loose shirt without a collar, a pair of linen trousers and old slippers with rope soles. Standing on the edge of the pond with his hands on his hips, he observed the water in silence. After a while he went inside and returned with a bucket and a long stick with a net on the end.

'The fish have grown big,' he said.

As soon as he sank the net in the water, the fish rushed to hide under the lilies.

'Do they taste any good?' the schoolmaster asked while marking the coursework.

The Arab shook his head and continued to plough the water with his net.

'Too many bones. They're only good for the mayor's cat.'

'I don't see why you look after that useless feline. She can't even catch a lame rat.'

Yusuf shrugged.

'Where I come from, cats are sacred,' he said. 'They're not tools.'

The schoolmaster did not raise his head from his work.

'Uh-huh.'

Catching a goldfish in murky waters was a challenge, especially with the Arab's bad back. He narrowed his eyes and steered the net towards an orange silhouette under the surface. He stopped humming, held his breath and struck. A pigeon sitting on the garden wall took flight with a few beats of its wings. Yusuf raised his net slowly: a large goldfish writhed in it. He looked closely at its scales and gave a smile that exposed his marvellous teeth.

'You're too fat to pass through the gates of Paradise,' he said, shaking his head with disapproval.

'But not too fat for the cat's mouth,' the schoolmaster said from where he sat.

Yusuf threw the fish into the bucket and lowered the net into the pond again. He asked casually, 'Is it true the mayor is going to marry Madame?'

On the margin of an answer sheet the schoolmaster wrote:

If the distance between the two bodies increases then their force of attraction should decrease as the square of that distance. He capped his pen and took off his glasses.

'Ha. It'd be inappropriate for a man of such a high office to associate himself with a fallen woman,' he said.

The Arab accepted the schoolmaster's argument but held the prostitute in high regard.

'She's a fallen angel,' he said. 'But the mayor has the face of a donkey.'

'Under her auspices he will run a formidable election campaign,' the schoolmaster said bitterly.

The rumours about the wedding kept him awake at night. The truth of the matter was that he worried he would lose Violetta for ever. As he raised the tube of the *narghile* to his lips, a butterfly entered the garden. His eyes followed its flight among the shrubs with sentimentality. Soon the attendant of the baths gave up trying to catch the goldfish and leaned on the rod of his net.

'I remember the day she arrived,' the Arab said. 'I thought she was the Queen of Sheba.'

Mr Othon had not forgotten either. The Frenchwoman had come to the town eleven years earlier, in the sacred hours of the afternoon rest, in a landau pulled by two water buffalo. Dressed only in his trousers and undershirt, the schoolmaster had walked on to his balcony in time to see a head covered by a hat trimmed with flowers come out of the window of the carriage. Violetta had stretched her neck, adorned with several diamond chokers, and sniffed the air. She had grimaced.

'*Ah non,*' she had said in the silence of the afternoon. '*Une autre ville qui sent la merde.*'

She had nevertheless instructed the driver to take down her luggage with care. The schoolmaster had watched from his balcony that overlooked the town square. To this day he remembered her embroidered bolero sewn with pearls, the purse and chatelaine draped around her waist, and when she lifted her skirt for her foot to find the step, the inch of three petticoats she wore underneath. As soon as she was on firm ground, she had pulled out a handkerchief from her cuff and sprinkled it with cologne. Having purified her pale cheeks from the miseries of the journey, she had told her maid: '*Annina, ma petite, on est arrivé chez nous.*'

In the shade of the garden Mr Othon fingered the mouthpiece of the *narghile*.

'The Queen of Sheba indeed,' he said. 'The problem with you Turks is that you're excessively sentimental.'

Yusuf grinned. He knew the affection the schoolmaster felt towards the Frenchwoman. He shook his head and sank his net into the pond again.

'Not Turk, Mr Othon,' he said. 'I'm Arab.'

The grocer sat on the bench across the street from the baths and stroked his beard. He had decided to take a walk after lunch and had found himself in the streets behind the market. He caught sight of the schoolmaster coming out of the *hamam*.

'According to my wife, teacher,' he called from across the street, 'that establishment is the essence of Ottoman decadence.'

The schoolmaster crossed the earthen street and joined the grocer on the bench.

'Women are suspicious of anything that puts a smile on a man's face,' he replied. 'Even laughing gas.'

The grocer took out his watch: it was time to open the shop. The two men walked towards the town square through the alleyways of the Muslim Quarter. From the open doors came the noise of snoring. Somewhere a treadle started, and a sewing machine rattled in the afternoon like a distant train. Lizards crisscrossed the two men's path and climbed the whitewashed walls. A bead curtain at an open door was blown about by the wind. The alleyways were not wide enough for both men to walk side by side, so the grocer walked ahead. Behind him the schoolmaster paused to switch his briefcase to his other hand. The walls carried his panting away – a moment later he heard it somewhere behind him. He found his handkerchief and mopped his brow, admitting to himself the burden of having to wear a suit all year round.

'Is this is the quickest route?' he asked. 'One needs a ball of thread to find one's way out.'

'A straight line is not always the shortest distance,' the grocer said.

A whiff of cooked food passed through the mosquito screen of a kitchen window. The schoolmaster put his handkerchief back in his pocket and hastened to catch up with the grocer.

'Pythagoras would disagree, of course,' he said.

The grocery shop stood in a corner of the square opposite the Town Hall. It had a signboard that read THE CORNUCOPIA GROCERY above a wooden horn of plenty. The grocer unlocked the door and walked in. 'Watch your step, teacher,' he said. When he lit the lamp, the schoolmaster saw the reason for the warning. Mousetraps baited with cheese were scattered across the floor. The grocer put on his white smock. A cloud of flies circled the lamp that hung from the ceiling. The schoolmaster put down his briefcase and rubbed his back. His eyes followed the circling insects.

'Lord have mercy,' he said. 'I'm teaching centripetal force next week.'

The shop was well stocked, and its merchandise was neatly displayed. On a shelf behind the counter, loaves of bread were arranged in size. On a table were a coffee grinder and tin boxes with coffee beans. On the counter were two scales with their weights. Despite all the delicacies on display, one smell dominated the shop: it was coming from the barrel of salted cod. Standing behind the counter, the Armenian dissolved a spoon of baking soda in a glass of water and drank it. Then he offered the schoolmaster a seat.

'I hear the mayor is getting married,' he said, uncorking a brandy bottle.

'It's impossible,' Mr Othon said. 'A marriage is null and void without an Orthodox priest.'

From the window of the grocery they could see the dome of Saint Gregorius Theologus and its belfry, rising above the roofs of the town. Once the church had a devout priest, two psalmists, a sexton and a pious congregation. On the feast day of its patron saint, it held a week-long fair with food, music and strongmen from distant Asian lands. Then the priest had decided to visit the Church of the Holy Sepulchre in Jerusalem, a pilgrimage he had not lived to complete: he had died on seeing the walls of Jericho. The answer to the town's request for a new priest had come in a letter written in the hand of the Ottoman governor. He had been a moderate man, who had fond memories of the town fair he attended every year. He had developed a deep affection for his infidel but hospitable subjects. In his letter he explained the political situation in the Balkans and predicted the flood of Muslim refugees into Asia Minor following the end of the Great War, the defeat of the Empire, as well as the violence that this would cause between the Muslims and the local Christians. He admitted that it would be impossible for him to prevent it. But there was a solution: the town could distance itself from its religion. After a long discussion among themselves, the Christian towns-people had decided that the preservation of the flesh took precedence over the salvation of the soul: they had not insisted on their request for a new priest.

Years had passed since the church doors had been locked and its windows boarded up. The rats had made it their home. Having eaten everything inside, from the candles to the drapery of the altar and the carpets, they had begun to attack the shops. As a result, the mayor had bought a cat, but she preferred to perch on the windowsills of the Town Hall.

The grocer poured two brandies.

'A priest is the least of the mayor's worries. The next town is only three hours away, and there's an Orthodox church there.'

The schoolmaster took the glass without thanks and drank it.

'If there's a priest inside, he'll probably be swinging from the chandelier.'

The Armenian refilled his glass.

'Anyhow,' he said. 'The mayor is determined to get married. Whether by a priest or by an imam.'

The schoolmaster opened his mouth to answer, but the sound of hoofs on the cobblestones cut through the silence of the afternoon and stopped him short with its urgency.

The lobby of the Town Hall was a huge room laid with tiles. A double flight of sweeping steps led up to a gallery of offices. Time had stripped off most of the lacquer from the doors, and the cedar-of-Lebanon wood gave off an ancient fragrance. On one door a handwritten sign read *I am not in*, but there was snoring coming from the other side.

Sitting at his desk with a pillow behind his head, the mayor paused to gulp in his sleep and continued to snore. On the windowsill, under the pane that vibrated to the noise, his cat also slept, lying on her side. The mayor opened his eyes and rolled his head in the direction of the window. A row of blossoming tamarisks stood in the courtyard round a marble bust. All night the wind had shaken the trees, and now the square was a sea of pink flowers. Two men were crossing the square, knee deep in the blossoms. The mayor recognised the Armenian and the schoolmaster.

The air in the office was hot. Still dazed with his slumber, he looked around. The flaking paint, the chipped pilasters and crazed tiles caused him a fleeting melancholy. The small town had managed to escape the war but had suffered nevertheless. Since the landing of the Expeditionary Corps, state funding had been suspended, and for the last two years the treasury remained empty. The mayor rubbed his nape. Why did living have to be so difficult? He stood up and went to the other end of his office, where two easy chairs were arranged on either side of a mahogany Victrola. A stack of dusty phonograph records was on the floor, and he riffled through it. He put one on, turned the crank and waited for the music to start before he returned, humming, to his desk. On the windowsill the cat yawned, stretched her legs and began to meow. The mayor gave her a brief glance and opened a drawer. A quick search under a pile of letters revealed a smoked herring wrapped in the obituaries of a Levantine newspaper. He sliced off the head and tail with a paperknife and gave them to the cat. He wiped the paperknife on his trousers, licked his fingers and wrapped the rest of the fish back in the newspaper.

'A meal not fit for a queen perhaps,' he said, stroking the cat. 'But fit for a bureaucrat at least.'

She was an Abyssinian with a red coat and a white chin. The mayor had bought her via mail order, having studied first an illustrated book of cats in the town library. While she ate he observed her with affection. In a moment the door opened and his secretary entered with a pencil stuck behind his ear. He looked at his boss stroking the cat and puffed.

'That animal has domesticated its owner,' he said.

He sneezed and started sniffing. While he was wiping his nose with his handkerchief, his eyes began to fill with tears.

'Cats are the proof that the Devil exists,' he said and went to open the balcony door. The fresh air soothed his allergic reaction.

The mayor did not take his eyes from the cat.

'Her ancestry goes back to the time of the Pharaohs,' he said.

In the square the wind shook the tamarisks, ruffled the sea of flowers and carried some petals through the open balcony door. Their vague fragrance covered the smell of the herring. The mayor thought about the state funerals he had attended over the years, where the same rose petals were used time after time to pave the way for the hearse. After a few ceremonies, the petals would become shrivelled and colourless like paper. When his mind landed again in reality, he noticed the music had ended. The needle of the Victrola was scratching the revolving record.

'Pharaohs or not, she's useless,' his secretary said. 'One of these days, the rats will spread the bubonic plague.'

The mayor went to switch off the Victrola.

'Now that the war is over,' he said, 'things will go back to normal, and we'll be able to afford to tear down the church.'

His secretary guffawed.

'Tear down the church? Are you serious?'

The mayor shrugged his shoulders.

'It's a source of pollution.'

The cat finished her food and meowed again. The mayor opened another drawer, took out a bottle of milk and filled her tray.

'Feed her as much as you like,' the secretary said. 'The Mameluke is her true master.'

The mayor frowned and pointed his finger in the direction of the baths.

'It has nothing to do with Yusuf. She goes there because the steam is good for her bones.'

The cat slurped her milk. When she had finished this too, she began to groom herself. The mayor lay back in his chair. Tapping his fingers on his desk, he remembered the damage done by the storm.

'Tell me what has been done about the roof,' he said.

His secretary put his hand in his pocket and took out a folded piece of paper. The mayor pouted.

'You call that a memorandum? You ought to start acting like a civil servant.'

'My ancestry doesn't go back to the time of the Pharaohs,' the secretary said.

A few days earlier, a sudden rainstorm had flooded the streets, the shops and the houses. The torrent had found its way into the abandoned church. From the clefts in the wall and the holes in the floor rats poured out in an endless flow and made their way to higher ground. They climbed above the spandrels of the church doors, past the parapets, and in their panic they did not stop when they reached the safety of the roofs or the dome but continued, squeaking and clawing, towards the belfry. Draped in rodents the church had been an ugly sight, but the real damage had happened some time later when the wind had damaged the warehouse of the Co-operative Association. The beams had snapped, and the roof had caved in. A column of air had blown the bales of tobacco leaves out of the warehouse, in the direction of the plain.

'According to my calculations,' the secretary said, 'we lost one-third of the crop.'

The mayor gave a sigh of relief.

'If the storm had lasted a little longer, we'd have to go down to the coast and beg for handouts,' he said.

'That would have been purposeless. Following the end of the war, those hands that aren't cut off are busy scraping the bottom of the barrel.'

He looked in the direction of the balcony door with an idle intention, but an unusual sight caught his attention: a chestnut horse was trotting round the square, cutting furrows in the tamarisk flowers with its hoofs. From outside the grocery, the schoolmaster and the Armenian watched it too. In a moment windows and doors opened, and other men and women stood and observed the horse in silence. It had no tack on, and when it passed under the balcony of the Town Hall, the secretary noticed to his horror that its croup was branded with the emblem of the Expeditionary Corps.

94

9

He uncorked the bottle and filled his glass. When he raised the drink to his lips, his fingers began to tremble, and he spilled it on the table. He waited for the shakes to subside, licked his fingers and refilled the glass. He sipped his raki carefully, observing the street from behind the window. The room was furnished frugally: a table and chair, a bed with a spring mattress, a washbasin, a chest of drawers. On the wall a mirror hung under a crucifix. A shared lavatory was at the end of the corridor. The shut windows preserved the humidity of that afternoon's sleep. Outside the wind blew briefly. Dangling from the balcony that faced the street, each tied with a piece of rusted wire, a row of blue tin letters tinkled: HÔTEL SPLENDIDE. The grandeur of the sign was not enough to disguise the advanced dilapidation of the small hotel. The war correspondent let out a sigh.

He was unshaven, with spiny stubble and tousled hair. He emptied his glass and refilled it. The end of the war was the worst thing that could have happened to him. A few weeks earlier, he was on his way to the front, riding on the back of a cart, when the news of the collapse had met him at this town. It had been unwise to spend a whole week in Izmir playing roulette. Not only had he parted with most of his savings but he had also lost the chance to witness the battle that tilted the scales of the war. He had lodged at the local hotel and taken to the bottle.

Once, he had been a cultural correspondent for a popular

national magazine. During the war he had watched with envy his colleagues leave for Asia Minor and later read their articles that reported the early victories of the Expeditionary Corps. Soon every one of these men had become famous. He had resigned, taken out all his savings from the bank and booked his passage to Izmir too.

He sipped his raki, while his eyes wandered about the room. The truth was that he had nothing to go back to. On top of the wardrobe a spider was slowly wrapping its web round his typewriter. On a ledge on the wall his Autographic Kodak lay open, its bellows and lens gathering dust. He finished his drink and hitched up his braces. Under the bed was a cardboard suitcase tied with a piece of rope he had not undone since his arrival in town. He put his shoes on his naked feet and left the room. In the lobby he came across the hotelier entering with a folded umbrella under his arm and a shopping net in his hand. The man stopped on the threshold and greeted his customer with a smile before cleaning his shoes on the scraper.

'Flowers!' he said cheerfully. 'The autumn is drowning us in rotten flowers!'

Watching the man trying to remove the petals stuck under his soles, the war correspondent felt the need for another drink. The distant hills had already begun to hide the sun. It was a warm evening. The town was built on the edge of the plateau, where the earth was rich in mineral salts. The war correspondent walked towards the centre of town. As soon as the square came into view, he thought he had slept through a carnival: the thick carpet of flowers stretched from the Town Hall to the shops opposite. A large crowd was gathered around a horse. The mayor was bending down behind its croup.

'No, it's male,' he said. 'It's been gelded.'

The crowd murmured. It had been a while since the armistice had been signed and both sides' prisoners had returned home. The journalist wondered what the army horse was doing there. Someone suggested it had survived the collapse of the front and wandered the plains for weeks. That would have been impossible. There was little food and water in the plains, but the animal appeared well fed. Also, it could not have escaped the jackals for so long. The war correspondent sat at the *lokanta* to solve the mystery. A moment later the mayor approached him.

'I understand you have a photographic apparatus,' he said.

The war correspondent sipped the first drink of the evening.

'It's true,' he said.

'Then you ought to take our picture with the horse.'

'The film's not cheap.'

The mayor took up a collection among the crowd and returned with a handful of coins.

'Move them close together while I fetch the camera,' the journalist said.

The townspeople gathered together, flattened their hair, folded their arms and stared at the lens with seriousness. Someone brought a rope, tied it round the horse's neck and gave it to the mayor. He held the rope firmly and nodded for the photographer to take the picture.

Annina was late in preparing Madame Violetta's dinner. She left the square in a hurry and cut across the Muslim Quarter. She found her way in the alleys easily, scraping through the tight clefts between the adobe walls, hidden by the shadows of the last daylight. She paused only once to find a pin in her pocket and fix a loose strand of her hair. She was a woman who dismissed her own beauty. There were more pins in her hair than spines on a hedgehog, she wore no jewellery, she used no cosmetics save for olive oil soap, and her bosom was trapped under a corset thick like a breastplate. She had been offered the job of a maid on the condition that she dressed like a nun. When Madame had taken her into service, she had also had to change her name, at the request of her mistress, to Annina, after a character from Madame Violetta's favourite opera. She had later discovered that Violetta was also the name of the protagonist of *La Traviata* and assumed her employer did not go by her real name either.

Walking down the alleyways of the Muslim Quarter, the maid thought about the unfairness of life. The dome of the abandoned church towered above the roofs of the town. Annina gave it a long look. She still believed in God but thought of Him as an incompetent alchemist. A smell of excrement blew from the direction of the open sewer that surrounded the town slum like a moat and made her pinch her nose.

She was grateful to her mistress for taking her on but did not approve of Madame's occupation. Even during the worst times of her fate, she herself had not forsaken her virtue. There had been opportunities to do so when she lived in the streets and even more afterwards while working for Madame Violetta in Paris: the doctor who used to treat her mistress; the retired general, a hero of the battle of Verdun, with the castor fixed to his peg-leg; the ambassador whose country, as Annina understood it, had ceased to exist after the Great War. They had all been buffoons. A brief sense of pride for a moment cancelled her virtue.

She came out of the alleyways. Madame's house could be seen ahead, beyond the shops on both sides of the street. The storm had carried away many tiles from the roof and exposed the rafters. She should not forget to ask Yusuf to replace them.

It was a two-storey white stucco house with tall French windows and big balconies. Two lines of defence protected its interior against the sun and the eyes of the townspeople: when the shutters were open to air the rooms, heavy curtains were drawn across the windows. In the front garden, persimmon trees stood among ornamental annuals. The maid closed the gate and stopped briefly to smell the roses. She normally entered the house through the kitchen door; sharing the main entrance with her mistress's clients made her uncomfortable. In the back garden, a man was weeding.

'Were you in the square?' Annina said.

'I wanted to be in the picture,' the Arab said and dug his hoe with frustration. 'But the mayor didn't let me in.'

The woman felt sorry for him.

'Where do you think the horse came from?'

'I'm sure there's an explanation.'

'The roses up front smell wonderful. You can raise the dead, Yusuf.'

The gardener shrugged.

'The secret is the dung. The rule is, the more shit you add, the better the fragrance.'

'Whatever it is, you could build the Hanging Gardens of Babylon.'

'Maybe,' the gardener said. 'If only I was given the money.'

'When Madame marries, you'll be able to buy all the flowers you want.'

'You mean the dung.'

'That too.'

Yusuf shook his head in doubt.

'The mayor's fist is as tight as a cork in a bottle.'

'It's not his money he'll be spending but the town's,' the woman said.

The Arab beamed at the thought and showed his perfect teeth.

'Then I'll dig a pond too and plant water lotus. To remind me of home and the great River Nile.'

The woman looked around her: there was no one. She reached out and touched the gardener's hump.

'Sweet Yusuf,' she whispered. 'What will happen to us?'

'*Allahu akbar*,' the Arab replied. 'If not, we're in trouble.'

99

He continued to weed with his hoe, and she watched him, neither of them saying a word. After a while the man spoke up.

'Are you coming tonight?'

The young woman nodded in reply and walked away in a hurry. As soon as she entered the kitchen, she heard her mistress's voice.

'. . . *Peut-être d'un injuste effroi ma tendresse est alarmée / Écoute, amour, et dis-moi, si je suis encore aimée.*'

When Annina shut the kitchen door, the song stopped briefly.

'Annina?'

The maid bit her lip. She was concerned about her mistress discovering her affair with Yusuf. She should not have been: it was not the first time that Violetta had watched the couple from her bathroom. She was a more tolerant person than she would let others know. While Annina examined her clothes and hair in front of the vestibule mirror, the song upstairs resumed.

'. . . *Un seul objet avait rempli mon âme je ne voyais / Que lui dans ce vaste univers.*'

There was a knock on the door, and the maid entered. A cast-iron bath as big as a rowing boat, coated with vitrified enamel and sitting on four lion paws, dominated the room. On its side was stamped the manufacturer's logo: *L. Wolff & Co., Chicago.* Violetta stretched her neck and looked at her employee like an ostrich then disappeared again under the rim of the bath.

'*Grâce à Dieu,*' she said. 'You're back. When my husband went for a walk, seventeen years ago, he forgot to return.'

The bath had been the mayor's engagement present to Violetta. He had discovered it under the cobwebs at the back of a second-hand shop in Izmir. It had cost him only a letter in which he informed the central government that the large sum received before the war for the construction of a covered conduit for the sewage had been diverted to fund an alternative sanitary project. He had not mentioned that this project was a new bath that did not leak for his bride-to-be.

Annina sat on a stool opposite Madame.

'I was detained in the square, Madame. A—'

'Fetch my brush, please.'

The maid handed the brush to her mistress and began to tell her about the army horse. Scratching her back with the brush, Violetta showed little interest.

'The mayor was there too,' Annina said. 'He took a collection to have our photo taken by that journalist who stays at the hotel.'

Her mistress dipped the brush in the water and continued her cleansing routine.

'That man has put his face in more pictures than Jesus,' she said about the mayor.

'You shouldn't talk that way about your future husband,' Annina said.

The Arab passed under their window with a saw. Violetta listened to him pruning the trees.

'For an enamelled bath I'd even marry our hunchback,' Annina blushed.

'Monsieur Yusuf is a fine gentleman.'

Violetta dropped the brush and picked up the sponge. She squeezed it over her back and felt the soap trickling down her shoulders.

'*D'accord*. A gentleman. But with the back of a camel nevertheless.'

Her maid said nothing.

'What do you call a camel with one hump?' her mistress asked.

'A dromedary, Madame.'

'*Un dromadaire*. But of course.'

Violetta poured water over her shoulders and began to sing again.

'. . . *Mais je sens qu'elle approche et va finir mes peines / Le poison des douleurs a coulé dans mes veines.*'

She stood up and washed off the lather from the rest of her body. When she finished she snapped her fingers to summon her maid's attention.

'*Allons, ma petite.* My robe.'

The moment she took the bathrobe, the doorbell began to ring. Violetta checked the time on the clock on the wall.

'*Putain,*' she sighed. 'I can't stand these rustics. Soon they'll be calling on us at breakfast.'

Annina placed the stool next to the tub so that her mistress could step out. Then she made a move to answer the door. Madame Violetta stopped her.

'Leave it. Whoever it is, he'll go away.'

She dried herself in her bathrobe and changed into a silk kimono. She pulled out the hairpins that held her hair up and sat at her vanity unit to put on her make-up. All the while the bell did not stop ringing.

'See who it is,' she said eventually, in a tone which suggested that she knew the answer. A moment later Mr Othon stood at the bathroom door, panting from having climbed the stairs. Violetta did not turn to look at him. She finished combing her hair and picked up the powder puff. The schoolmaster watched her with disapproval.

'See if dinner is ready, *jolie,*' Violetta said.

As soon as he was alone with Violetta, the schoolmaster tried to hug her, but she pushed him away. He took a few steps back and ran his fingers along the lip of the bath.

'Your thirty pieces of silver,' he said with contempt.

The woman opened her blusher set.

'What are you doing here? You know you're not welcome.'

'I remember, not long ago, how you used—'

'Things have changed.'

'*Sic transit gloria mundi,*' the schoolmaster said.

Violetta sighed.

102

'You know how speaking Latin bores me,' she said.

Mr Othon came closer.

'There's no reason why we shouldn't preserve our discreet *association*, under the changing circumstances,' he said and rested his hand on the woman's shoulder. 'To our mutual benefit, of course.'

Violetta turned round and hit him across the face with the blusher brush.

'*Ce n'est pas une façon de s'adresser à l'épouse d'un représentant de l'état, Monsieur!*'

The brush left some blusher on Mr Othon's cheek. The fact that he had no French and had understood not a word only added to his fury.

'So be it,' he said. 'The forces of evil have won. I wish you both a harmonious matrimony. Only remember this, my sweet. When—'

Suddenly they heard the sound of a distant drum. They turned silent and listened to the beat, a slow tempo less suitable for a military march than a funeral. Ever since the harmony teacher had left to invest his savings in a plantation in the Belgian Congo, Mr Othon had also taught music at the school. Out of habit he tried now to determine the metre of the march. The playing was erratic, almost childish: it was the way an untrained pair of hands would play – or an exhausted one. They could not tell where it was coming from. For a moment the schoolmaster had the impression the sound was blowing over from the direction of the plain. He quickly dismissed the idea – it would have been impossible, there was no one out that way. He noticed that the sound was coming closer. Suddenly the maid called from the other side of the door: '*Madame! Madame!*'

Tying the string of her kimono, Violetta opened the door. Annina waved to her to come to the window. Mr Othon followed them nervously.

'What is it, *ma petite*?' Violetta asked.

The maid only had to pull the heavy curtain aside for her mistress to get her answer. As soon as her eyes adapted to the twilight, the Frenchwoman saw them: a long file of soldiers on foot and some on horseback, stretching back to the distant hills was entering the town, their uniforms, boots and faces covered with dust.

10

The midday sun cast the skewed shadows of a riddle of crosses on the floor. Round the room the furniture stood anyhow, covered with dustsheets: chairs, cabinets, a marble conference table. Beyond the shut windows, the world was warm and silent. Soldiers strolled across the town square with their rifles slung over their shoulders. If they happened on an officer, they looked down. The officer would do the same and walk on towards his quarters, where he would lie down, away from the eyes of his men and the glare of the sun through the windows and write another letter home it was impossible to post.

Brigadier Nestor paced round the marble table. He was alone in the room. He had every reason to feel content. The brigade had escaped death many times: the heat, the thirst, the enemy. And now salvation – almost. There was food and fresh water in the town, and the sea – at last they knew for certain – was not far. But Brigadier Nestor felt in fact something akin to despair.

Outside a cart rolled by, tearing up the afternoon silence like paper. The smell of oleander came from the corners of the conference room: someone had recently sprinkled it with rat poison. There were dried ink stains on the floor. His cot was set among the furniture, together with his desk, his chair and his maps. Next to them lay his trunk with its lid open; shirts and trousers were scattered across the floor or hung down from the rim. He looked at his trunk and at last remembered.

He found his parade boots, poked his hand inside one and took out a small bottle. He lit a match and held the flame under the needle of the syringe to sterilise it. Then he filled the syringe and injected himself. Not waiting for the drug to take effect, he gave himself another shot in the other arm. Now he could rest.

He had taken up his residence in the Town Hall when the brigade arrived in the town three days earlier. Standing on the steps to the entrance, the mayor had welcomed him with a sentimental address that disguised deep suspicion. Together they had walked inside, where the mayor had insisted on giving him a tour of the building. On the ground floor, he was shown into the room that housed the municipal library. It had been a pleasant surprise. On the stacks, behind the dusty cobwebs, arranged in alphabetical order, was a forgotten treasure. There were first editions of the classics, volumes by Alexandrian poets, a Ptolemaic Septuagint and parchments with maps that showed the Titan Atlas bearing the Earth on his back. The brigadier had forgotten his exhaustion and studied them with fascination. On the counter the lending register had lain open. His host had blown off the dust and run his finger down the ancient list of entries.

'The last person to borrow a book was Moses,' he had said. '*The Commandments*. According to this he never returned it.'

In another room Brigadier Nestor was shown the Byzantine icons brought to the Town Hall only days before a neighbouring monastery was destroyed by arsonists. Then his eyes had fallen on a top hat kept inside a glass cabinet. He had enquired about it.

'We bought it from a conjuror at the annual fair,' the mayor had explained, 'with the intention of starting a rabbit colony. But we haven't as yet managed to pull out a single one.'

He had then guided the officer in front of a wall of framed honorary diplomas, the awards from various international

106

trade fairs to the Co-operative Association for its tobacco. When they had reached the door of the conference room, the mayor tried to open it, but it had been locked. For a long time, they had searched for the key but failed to find it, so in the end they had had to break the lock. The furniture had been covered when the war had begun and the governor, declaring a state of emergency, had dissolved the council.

Brigadier Nestor fell on a chair and was covered in a cloud of dust. He contemplated his naked arms, scarred by the needle. He shut his eyes to avoid the sight and recalled again the village massacre as clearly as the day he had ordered it. His conscience assured him that his crime would follow him wherever he went. For the first time since it had happened, he considered the likelihood of his shame outliving him. The thought pricked his heart. It was not vanity. He never cared for posterity; it was his legacy to his grandson he worried about.

He thought, the enemy of course knows what has happened, but our academicians could easily dismiss that as propaganda. The real problem was his own troops. Sooner or later there was bound to be some soldier who would talk. Then it would be only a matter of time before the press got hold of the story. But what if the brigade never made it to the sea? He thought carefully about the possibility. He had little to lose himself. How many more years would he live? Two, three, five perhaps: a blink of the eye at his age. Suddenly the possibility of coming across the enemy lost some of its dread.

The creak of the door startled him, and he reached for his pistol. Despite the large dose of morphia, his instinct had not completely abandoned him. It was only his orderly.

'A civilian insists on seeing you, sir.'

Brigadier Nestor relaxed his grip on his revolver.

'One of these days you will scare me to death, son,' he said. 'If you're lucky, that is. Because I might shoot you by mistake.' The room draped the two men in its gloomy light. 'Anyway. Who is it? That mayor again?'

His orderly handed him a creased calling card. Brigadier Nestor took out his glasses to study the coat of arms printed on it: a shield with an open scroll underneath that read *Lux in Tenebris*. The brigadier pursed his lips.

'Light in darkness,' he said. 'Just the thing we need in this room.' He removed his glasses. 'Very well. Show him in.'

The journalist entered. Brigadier Nestor waved his orderly away and sized up his visitor. The war correspondent introduced himself.

'The fourth estate,' Brigadier Nestor said. 'Even in the pits of Hell there's bound to be one of you reporting back.'

'His name was Dante Alighieri,' the journalist said.

His appearance that afternoon bore no resemblance to the man in Hôtel Splendide a few days earlier. His cheeks were smooth after a long hot towel treatment, his hair was combed with perfumed ointment and his fingernails manicured. His resurrection at the hands of the local barber could only have been achieved on credit. Brigadier Nestor clasped his hands behind his back and walked up to a window.

'Dante, eh? A genius of allegory,' he said. 'Not many of our people are familiar with the Italian poet.'

'I grew up with Italian poetry,' the war correspondent said. 'We had to.'

'How's that?'

'Our family name is included in the Register of Nobility of the Venetian Republic,' the journalist said.

He was a native of the Ionian Islands. While the rest of the country had been conquered by the Ottomans, the western archipelago had had the relative good fortune of falling into the hands of the Venetians. The near-benevolent occupation that had lasted almost four hundred years had infected the locals with a passion for culture and a streak of loftiness.

'What can I do for you?' the brigadier asked.

108

'I heard about your adventure and wanted to know how on earth you led your army through the wilderness.'

'Oh, it was Pegasus,' the brigadier said. 'I trust you're familiar with his story?'

'The mythical horse?'

'Correct. The winged horse, son of Poseidon and Medusa.'

The journalist did not understand until the brigadier narrated the events that had led to their salvation. About the gelding which someone had let loose on the night of the storm, and how the horse and the detail sent to bring it back in order not to give away their position to the enemy had chanced upon the town that had proved the exit from the labyrinth. Brigadier Nestor paced up and down, the walls echoing back the sound of his boots on the parquet.

'If I catch the man who freed the horse,' he said, 'I won't know whether to shoot him or decorate him.'

'I see. Your soldiers followed the horse's tracks.'

'Technically the trail of shit,' Brigadier Nestor said. 'Because the wind swept the tracks away but not the dung.'

He recounted the other events of their journey, mentioning also the incidences of theft. He dropped his voice to a whisper.

'I believe the thief and the man who freed the horse are the same person.'

The war correspondent nodded.

'There's also the matter of the handbills,' he said.

Brigadier Nestor frowned.

'You seem well informed. Perhaps you know things I don't?'

The journalist shrugged.

'Nothing more than what your soldiers say. Do you think the agitator is the thief?'

'My instinct says no. But at this stage, I exclude no possibility.'

'One way or another, it's an extraordinary story.'

109

Brigadier Nestor felt uncomfortable. He wondered, with dread, whether the journalist knew about the massacre too.

'I'm glad you find it entertaining, my friend,' he said.

The journalist smiled.

'Not just me, my brigadier. After this terrible defeat, the return home of your lost army will be a marvellous event.'

'Marvellous, yes,' the brigadier said. 'If we survive.'

'I mean it'll be an opportunity for the nation to feel proud again. I'll make sure of that if you let me be the brigade's official chronicler.'

Brigadier Nestor scratched his head.

'Well, you're the only journalist to ask so far.'

The war correspondent offered his hand.

'My brigadier,' he said. 'With your cooperation I promise to make you more famous than Odysseus of Ithaca.'

They shook hands. The more the old officer considered the idea, the more he liked it. If the brigade were to be depicted as a heroic army, then it would be in the journalist's interest, as much as the government's, to suppress any uncorroborated stories regarding the crime of the massacre. In addition, he himself would be venerated. It would be a great legacy for his family. Thinking about all this, Brigadier Nestor's mood began to improve.

Despite its size the church of Saint Gregorius Theologus was a melancholy sight: the silent belfry, the mossy steps, the locked doors. Father Simeon watched the sun hide behind the big dome and then walked away from the window. He studied the unfamiliar surroundings. He was billeted with the Armenian grocer and his wife. On the table were his altar cross, a censer, a stack of pages hooked on a piece of wire: the remnants of his copy of the Scriptures. Despite it being a proper house, the place reminded him less of his home than his tent had. On the wall, hanging in prominence, was a portrait of a grandmother in a heavy gilded frame. A stuffed eagle, frozen in mid-flight, eyed him with its glass-bead eyes. Father Simeon went downstairs to the kitchen. Behind a pall of steam, the Armenian woman was preparing dinner.

'You look like an alchemist,' the padre joked.

The woman came and kissed his hand. Father Simeon blessed her.

'Please go back to your work,' he said. 'It smells very good.'

'Men don't know that pleasure can be found even in the heart of an artichoke,' the woman said.

Father Simeon was uncertain how to respond. He agreed that carnality was the quickest route to damnation, but what the woman was saying seemed to promote the sin of gluttony.

'Yes,' he said. 'But the iniquities of the flesh include those of the stomach too.'

The woman shrugged her shoulders and leaned over her pot. Father Simeon looked at the wall clock with Mount Ararat painted on its dial. He admired the hand of the traditional artist but not his knowledge of history: stranded on the snow-capped peak was a ship with smoking funnels. He decided to go for a walk. Tamarisks lined the roadsides, but the colour of their flowers was lost in the dusk. The signs above the shop windows were illegible. He approached a house with white stucco walls that was surrounded by a big garden. The smell of jasmine offered him a brief relief from his gloom. Lost in his thoughts, he wandered towards the slum on the outskirts of town.

The first shadow appeared on a wall not far from where he stood. It moved from one house to the next, pausing for a moment at each door. Soon it was joined by another and then another until the alleys resonated with whispers. Father Simeon shuddered. When they came nearer, he saw that the people were barefoot and dressed in rags.

They did not see him. Father Simeon soon realised that they were scavenging for food but also for rubbish to repair and sell back to their neighbours in the town. The padre watched them walk back and forth, carrying split stovepipes, old machinery parts, cooking pots and broken earthenware. Children loitered about a group of soldiers, begging a coin or a cigarette. Surrounded by the spectacle of destitution, Father Simeon felt a transformation take place inside him.

'I thought it was the retreat,' he said. 'But, after all, this is meant to be my true road to Damascus.'

The crowd looked at him and went about its trade.

'Friends,' he called.

They paid no attention to him. Father Simeon convinced himself that this was his lost flock. He could, at last, become the missionary of the dream of his youth. He tried the words quietly: Apostle of All Anatolians. It sounded good. He went towards them.

'Listen to me,' he called again. 'In the name of God.'

Three men carrying an iron bedstead over their heads stopped and looked in his direction. The padre waved at them.

'I need your help,' he said. 'Come with me. There's profit to be gained. Believe me.'

He set off in a hurry. They followed him to the church, where another obstacle waited. Father Simeon could not force open the heavy doors. It was the crowd that showed him how to get in, through an opening in the walls. The secret passage led them into the sacrarium.

'Back,' the padre said. 'This is the Holy of Holies, and only a priest has the right to enter.'

They obeyed. Father Simeon asked for a lantern and explored the sacrarium alone. Over the years the church had been plundered meticulously. The altar table was still there, but he could find nowhere either the tabernacle or the Gospel. He ran his hand along the dusty tabletop.

'We have to invite the Lord back to this place,' he said.

What the looters had left behind had been damaged by time. The altarpiece had been one of the first items to be dismantled and carried away, but the bishop's throne was still there, its canopy torn. Only a few broken pews had been left behind, a psalmist's lectern and the largest of the candelabra, which now lay on the floor. Father Simeon surveyed the nave in silence. When he came to the narthex, he could not suppress his horror: the baptismal font was brimming with rats. He sat on the steps of the Royal Doors and thought about the restoration of Saint Gregorius Theologus. A moment later he was tapped on the shoulder and handed something. His fingers recognised it before the light of a lantern confirmed it: heavy and immaculate, the Gospel lit up his face with the glow of its gilding. The scavengers had long saved it from the rats. Father Simeon held it to his chest and his eyes watered.

'Thank you,' he said.

Then someone asked him, 'You want to buy it, priest?'

113

11

The mayor finished polishing the shoes and put them next to the rest of the uniform: the knee-socks with the green garters, the ironed shorts, the khaki shirt with the badges and pins, the blue scarf, the broad-brimmed hat. He inspected the items arranged on his desk and began to undress. He put his civilian clothes on the hanger and tried to fit into the shorts. He heard the door opening behind him.

'There ought to be an age limit to being a Scout,' a voice said. 'Or at least a weight one.'

The mayor did not turn. He breathed in and quickly buttoned his flies. His skin was pale and covered with tufts of dense hair. He buckled on his belt and breathed out.

'Who let you in?' he asked.

The schoolmaster closed the door and went towards the Victrola.

'As a public servant, your door ought to be open to all the Sultan's subjects.'

'Haven't you heard? The Empire is no more.'

'Even more so in a republic.'

The mayor sighed. The war had sped up the collapse of the Ottoman Empire and brought about a state of affairs whose novelty scared him. The truth was that the military expedition in Asia Minor had pulled the carpet from under his feet. He missed the past.

'A republic.' he said. 'I want to know what genius first came up with the idea of elections.'

114

Mr Othon lifted the cover of the Victrola and looked in. 'Our wise ancestors.'

The mayor picked up his scarf and tied it over his shoulders.

'That doesn't necessarily make it a good idea,' he said. 'The ancients also thought the sun was a man riding a chariot.'

After a quick search through the stack of records, the schoolmaster placed one on the turntable and turned the crank. He contemplated the rotating record with his hands in his pockets. Standing in front of the mirror, the mayor put on his Scout's hat.

'Are you still planning to run for office?' the schoolmaster asked.

'It's too early in the day to talk politics.'

'Naturally. You have more important things to consider first.'

'That is correct.'

The mayor searched for his Scoutmaster's cane. It was not in the drawers of his desk or in the filing cabinet. Mr Othon watched him with spite.

'I still think of you as my friend, Othon,' the mayor said. 'Do you see my cane anywhere?'

He looked in the closet with the cleaning materials. His cane was under the dustpan. He brushed it against his shorts and held it under his arm while adjusting his garter. A pain in his spine reminded him of his age. He had joined the Scouts ten years earlier. The humanitarian ideals of the Movement had stirred the last dregs of his integrity, and he had fallen passionately for it. He had created a large troop from the boys in the town and organised outdoor activities. The schoolmaster had joined up briefly too, but the prospect of spending his Sundays in the company of his students had soon made him drop out.

The mayor still revelled in it. Having read about the first Scout jamboree in London, he was saving up in order to

115

attend the next with some of the boys. But his engagement to Madame Violetta meant that he might have to postpone his trip: his fiancée wanted a child.

'Some friend,' said the schoolmaster.

'I asked you to be my best man, didn't I?'

'Fuck off!'

'In my schooldays teachers used to swear in Latin.'

The schoolmaster clenched his teeth.

'You and that suffragist, that French—!'

The mayor pointed his cane at the door.

'I'm afraid public hours are over. I have a matter to attend to.'

He left the room ahead of his former friend. In the square a contingent of Scouts waited for him in the sun. He searched his pockets for his whistle. Battered by the winds, the tamarisks on either side of the street stood naked. Their flowers had been swept off the square and piled up against the walls, the thresholds and drains, rotting. A few birds sat on the branches of the trees. The mayor shuddered at the sensation of the changing season. He blew his whistle, and the Scouts lined up, holding their staffs at their sides. When they were ready, he gave the Scout salute, clasped his hands behind his back and began his inspection.

The boys' uniforms were starched and ironed. One boy carried the toy drum the mayor had bought some time ago from the ringmaster of an Armenian circus. The drum had belonged to Hieronymus, a mercurial macaque which had escaped the circus and found refuge in a nearby *madrasa*. The mayor had heard that the animal's flight had to do with the ringmaster and the sin of sodomy. He frowned at a boy whose shirt was missing a button and continued, tapping his cane against his palm. He completed his review and returned to the middle of the line-up.

'Attention, Scouts,' he ordered. 'Recite the Pledge.'

The boys chanted: 'On my honour I pledge that I will do

my best to do my duty to God and the King, to help other people at all times and to obey the Scout Law.'

The mayor nodded with satisfaction.

'Who's the standard-bearer today?'

A boy came forward. Observing him with pride, the mayor tried to reconcile his embezzler's guilt with the ideals of the Movement.

'The flag,' he said.

The boy took out a paper Turkish flag he had sketched and coloured himself and pinned it to his staff. When the mayor saw it, he ran to take it.

'Fool,' he said. 'Do you want us all shot?'

The boy said, 'The other day you said we're proud citizens of the Turkish Republic now.'

'That was before the soldiers came,' the mayor said.

He sent the boy to bring a Greek flag and glanced at his watch: the brigadier was late for the parade. A while later he heard the distant noise of an exhaust. Soon an officer in a dusty uniform arrived on an old postman's motorcycle. The mayor watched the arrival of the backfiring motorcycle with a frown.

'I was expecting the brigadier,' he said.

Major Porfirio dismounted and saluted.

'He sends his apologies. I'm his Chief of Staff. I'll be honoured to attend the festivities on his behalf.'

The mayor received the news with frustration. As the local representative of the Sultan, he was not used to his invitations being turned down. Another shortcoming of democracy, he thought. His gloom about the change of season intensified.

'The republic will never last,' he sighed. 'The bullet is faster than the ballot box.' He pushed back his hat and faced his troop of Scouts. 'Attention, Scouts! Dip the flag.'

Major Porfirio made an effort to salute the standard. The Scoutmaster called out another order. The noise of their feet startled the birds on the trees, and they flew off towards the church. The mayor blew his whistle again, and the young Scouts were set in motion to the sound of the toy drum. Watching them circle the square, the mayor felt proud. He guided his guest to the shade.

'The aim of the Movement is to provide opportunities for developing those qualities of character which make one a good citizen,' he said. 'Honour, self-discipline, self-reliance, willingness and ability to serve one's community.'

Major Porfirio contemplated the marching children with sadness.

'These are indeed the fundamental principles,' he said.

'It's what Plato has called an education in virtue from youth onwards,' the mayor continued. 'It makes a man want to be a perfect citizen by teaching him how to rule correctly and how to obey.'

'Oh yes, to obey,' Major Porfirio said. 'Of course.'

'The methods of Scouting are based on the natural desires of youth. By giving them practical and attractive outlets, it turns them to socially valuable purposes. The young Scout is unaware of what lies behind his training. To him it's just a game played with his comrades.'

The boys completed another circle round the square while the drum shooed away the birds. The mayor forgot his speech.

'Things used to run like clockwork before the war,' he said.

He blew his whistle, and the Scouts began to sing. But marching and singing at the same time was difficult to do, and they soon started to fall out of step. The mayor was embarrassed by the spectacle.

'This would be a fine town if only it were in Europe,' he said with sad eyes.

It was the major whom Air Lieutenant Kimon had seen setting free the horse, an offence that was not serious but strange. What else was this secretive man capable of? the airman thought. He raised his eyes to the evening sky and recalled the discussion that had taken place between him and the major some days earlier. He looked at the dust, the stones, the gravel of the street and longed for his biplane. Beyond the edge of the town, a dust storm hissed.

He examined his burns from the crash: they were healing slowly. The fire had burned his cheeks, the nape of his neck and hands. A fly touched down on his forehead but took off before his hand could crush it. It would be fun to see the major humiliated, he thought and continued his walk.

He heard a coo. A cage hung from the eaves of the grocery. Inside, four pigeons flopped about, stupefied by the heat. While he observed them with an empty mind, he felt the urge to urinate and walked towards the municipal park. As soon as he passed the gate, the birds, invisible in the dusk, broke into song. He unbuckled his trousers behind a large palm and directed his stream on to its trunk. When he finished he threw stones at the high branching spikes until he had collected enough dates. He ate with relish, and only when he finished did he notice that his actions had silenced the birds. The sweet fruit had made him thirsty, and he went to look for water. He took a path shaded by cypresses, which became narrower and darker the further he went, until he came to an iron gate wrapped in ivy: the town cemetery. The gate creaked on its hinges, and he walked across the dry poplar leaves that cracked under his boots. Everything was covered with moss: the stone crosses, the urns, the praying angels, the roofs of the mausoleums. Something moved across the fallen leaves – perhaps a snake or a bird. His eyes caught sight of a line of snails, and he followed them to a fountain filled with water. He skimmed the slime with his hand, and while he drank the songbirds began to sing again.

The great hero being taught a lesson, Air Lieutenant Kimon thought again – the major might even lose his place among the staff. At the far end of the cemetery, he saw the big house that was his destination. He entered via the back garden, making his way through the vines with the last grapes of the season, the lemon trees, the sprigs of coriander. In the house itself, the doors and windows were open, surrendering their curtains to the breeze. On the veranda a flowerpot lay in pieces. In the living room, the airman discovered the culprit: a cat was sitting in an armchair, clawing the upholstery. He leaned over a grand piano and fingered the keyboard. By the time he heard the steps behind him, he had convinced himself he should inform on the major.

A voice said, 'The only place one can listen to good music these days is in the brothel.' Brigadier Nestor brought a finger to his lips and grinned. 'Please don't tell the mayor you saw me. I'm supposed to be busy reviewing the artillery.'

Instead of attending the Scouts' parade, he had spent his morning under Madame Violetta's satin sheets. Air Lieutenant Kimon saluted him.

'My brigadier. I'd like a word, if you please.'

His superior checked his watch.

'Not now, son. I have an important appointment. Come and see me later.'

Ever since his arrival in the town, the brigadier had been hearing stories concerning the wife of the Armenian grocer, a necromancer whose reputation was known across the Levant. He was told that voices would echo across the room during her seances, various objects would come afloat, musical instruments would play spontaneously, carnations would materialise from her mouth. As soon as he had heard about it, the brigadier thought of his late wife: the medium could help him say the last farewell.

The Armenian grocer had been waiting at the door. His house stood on the tip of a forked street and was shaped like the prow of a ship. A small balcony filled with flowerpots jutted out from its narrow front, over a street lamp nailed into the wall. When he saw the officer, the grocer snuffed out his cigarette and put it in his pocket.

'You're very fortunate, my brigadier. Tonight is a new moon.'

'So?'

'Souls like darkness.'

The night moved slowly down the cobbled street, darkening the whitewashed walls one after another. The Armenian moved aside. Brigadier Nestor crossed the threshold and felt he was being transported to a mysterious world. His host picked up a lamp and shone it into the darkness.

'Follow me,' he said. 'But watch your step. There're spirits about. They've refused to return to the underworld after one of the seances, and it's difficult to get rid of them.'

He gave his customer a sidelong glance. The creaking of a door made Brigadier Nestor shiver. It was a large house, but after a few minutes he wondered whether they were walking in circles. They went up and down stairs, along corridors, through doors the Armenian would open with some key from the bunch on his belt and lock immediately behind them so that the wandering souls would not contaminate the rest of the house. Finally they reached a door at the top of a spiral staircase.

'My general,' a voice said when the two men entered. 'Welcome. Leave your authority outside and come in.'

'I'm your servant,' the brigadier said.

He removed his cap and coat and bowed with reverence. The medium's parlour was a circular room with dark drapery covering the walls. The woman was sitting behind a small table with a crystal ball on it.

'You may sit,' she said.

The grocer showed him to a chair and left.

'I hold no answers myself, General,' the woman began. 'I'm merely a servant of the spirits. It is they who will give you the answers you require.'

'But you who will receive the fee,' the brigadier said.

His host stared him out of his wit. Shrouded by a heavy

dress, her feet pressed the pedals of a secret machine under her chair. The table began to rise in the air, astonishing the brigadier. A moment later a whiff of perfume entered the parlour.

'State your name, spirit,' the necromancer said.

Her face began to distort. When she spoke again, her voice was huskier:

'*Conte Alessandro di Cagliostro.*'

She had chanced upon the infamous adventurer in a book she had borrowed from the municipal library. One of the countless charlatans for whom the Renaissance was to blame, the self-proclaimed count had excelled in anything from forgery to fortune telling. Posing as a physician, hypnotist or Freemason, he had travelled throughout Europe, peddling his elixirs of immortal youth. Eventually, he had been seized by the Inquisition and condemned to death as a heretic, but his sentence had been commuted to life imprisonment. Impressed by his story, the Armenian necromancer had made him her favourite conferee from the afterlife, but Brigadier Nestor was not pleased to make his acquaintance.

'I've come here to communicate with my wife, madam,' he reminded the medium.

'*You command your troops well, General. Let us see whether you would be as competent with the legions of demons too.*'

'You seem to speak our language fluently for a foreigner, count,' the brigadier said. 'Your syntax is impeccable and you appear to have no accent whatsoever.'

The spirit let that comment pass.

'*I bring greetings from a person who keeps you in the safe of her heart,*' it said through the medium.

Brigadier Nestor's mood turned sombre.

'You do? Tell her she's the love of my life. I cherished her and I always will.'

'*Cherish,*' the count said scornfully. '*You have committed adultery.*'

122

Brigadier Nestor shifted on his chair.

'Oh that. It was a long time ago. Back then I was—'

'*Repeatedly. All your long matrimonial life.*'

The officer bit his lip.

'Are you sure that this is Count Cagliostro, madam?' he asked. 'My mother-in-law happens to be dead, too.'

Suddenly the Armenian woman spoke in her own voice.

'Don't mock the proceedings, general. You may find that death rids one of one's humour.'

The senior officer complied. But since his meeting with the journalist, there had been something else he also meant to ask.

'Will I find fame, count?'

The medium's answer was prompt but ambiguous too:

'*Your achievements will one day be known to the world, general.*'

The prophecy brought the massacre to the brigadier's mind. It was one achievement he did not want the world to know about. He was still contemplating the answer when the spirit spoke again.

'*Beware, sir. Some vultures circle above your head. Others walk alongside you.*'

The brigadier pouted. Without a doubt the spirit was referring to the thief and the traitor.

'Who are they? Can you give me their names?'

By now he should have known that the Divine Cagliostro was not in the habit of offering straight answers.

'*A plain tunic conceals the truth well. One with insignia does it better.*'

Brigadier Nestor tried another question:

'Will we ever see our homes again?'

The spirit was about to oblige him again when gunshots were heard. The officer jumped out of his chair and drew his revolver. He left the room and the world of the spirits in a hurry, not waiting to hear the medium's answer.

12

The first time he had done it out of panic. When he had run out of host for the Eucharist, the cook had refused to help him. Since the beginning of the retreat, food had been rationed, and there were orders not to waste a single loaf of bread. But the cook had said that they could come to an understanding. So when one morning the brigadier was out on a scouting mission, the cook had sent the padre to steal the sugar. It had been easier than he had anticipated. The cross on his chest had been the master key to every door. When next the padre ran out of consecrated wine, it took him only a few seconds to persuade his conscience, and he had raided the Chief of Staff's private stock. After that came the medic's razor: he and the cook had become profiteers.

The only time things had gone awry was while he was searching for the brigadier's cigars. A snake had crept into the lorry and snapped its jaws an inch from his hand. He had crushed it under his heel before leaving some time later with the loot under his tunic. He now contemplated whether the serpent had perhaps had some ominous significance but quickly dismissed the pagan thought. He had absolved himself of guilt by arguing that what he stole were luxury items one should do without in normal life, let alone in a dire situation like the present. He would never have done anything that would have jeopardised the safety of the soldiers. His unorthodox practice was only meant to secure their salvation – the spiritual one, that is, the one that mattered the most.

Father Simeon heaved a sigh and hugged himself. It was cold inside the church of Saint Gregorius Theologus. After the discovery of the Gospel, he had left the Armenian couple's house and made the church his home. He threw another piece of wood on the fire that burned in the middle of the empty nave. The flaking murals on the walls stared down at him with stern eyes. Sparks took flight from his small fire and burned out a few feet above the ground. Squatting on the cold floor, the padre studied the stolen items from that night: a pair of riding boots with silver spurs and a ceremonial sabre with a tasselled cord on its scabbard. That morning he had heard that the brigadier would be passing the evening in the Frenchwoman's villa. It was the perfect opportunity. Ever since Father Simeon had touched the golden covers of the Gospel shown to him by the scavengers, he had vowed that the sacred book would be his. He had only to find the money.

He thought that the boots and sword ought to be enough to buy him the ancient Gospel but was prepared for obstinate haggling in the slum the following day. The fire was burning out, and he had no more wood left. He wrapped himself in his coat, leaned against one of the columns that supported the dome of the church and closed his eyes. Despite the cold he felt happy for the first time in months.

The night of the new moon was supposed to act in his favour, but the corporal could hardly see where he was going. He felt his heart beat. He had been waiting long for this moment, watching the waning moon with impatience every night. That evening it had at last disappeared. Apart from a patrol of soldiers, there was going to be no one else around. The bugle had long since sounded blackout. The street lamps had been put out, the curtains pulled across windows and the town sunk into darkness. The corporal had waited until the town clock had sounded midnight, and then he had set off. Moments like this he wished he were not a communist: a prayer would have given him strength. He went, nevertheless.

The absence of light meant that he had escaped his shadow, but the sound of his boots followed him, the walls echoing every step. He stopped and removed his boots, tied them together and hung them from his neck. He continued in his socks, less comfortably but more quietly, pricking up his ears. The only sound other than his heartbeat was the rustle of the tamarisks. Feeling around with his foot, he guessed he was in the market. He had noticed the cobblestone pavement before, but he did not know exactly where he was; it was impossible to read the signs. He had a map in his back pocket but could not read it in the dark. He concentrated: his quarters, the street that passed in front of the villa, the park. The square should be round the next corner.

But it was not. He stopped to catch his breath. Though he had only been walking, his chest swelled as if he had been drilling for hours. He smelled the open sewer and wondered whether he was heading for the slum. That was not on the route he had laid out for his escape. But it was too late to go back. He pushed on reluctantly, the brief calls of an owl adding to his agony. A moment later he admitted he was lost.

Apart from the map, he carried in his backpack the letters from his secret love in Salonika, a few tins of food, a blanket, bottles filled with water, a bayonet to defend himself and the Party's pamphlet explaining surplus value. His idea was that if he were captured by the enemy, the pamphlet could be his passport to freedom: he was an internationalist and a proletarian. He stopped, put down his backpack and listened. He thought he heard something. No, there was no one. He was preparing to start again when he saw it: a pair of yellow eyes. He stood still, and for a while nothing happened. But the moment he took a step, the padre's dog began to bark.

He ran. It was difficult with the weight on his back and the boots dangling from his neck, but he managed several hundred yards before he threw away his pack. Suddenly his plan was not to reach the coast any more; he would be happy to make it to the hills. Where was he? He turned sharply round a corner and immediately stumbled on an obstacle that must have been a flowerpot from the way it sounded when it broke to pieces. Still after him Caleb paused briefly, intrigued by the noise, and then continued his pursuit.

The dog was in high spirits. This was not what it had expected on such a cold night. As a matter of fact, there was very little to do in this town at any hour of the day. There was the cat it had spotted wandering from the *hamam* to the Town Hall and back, but no sooner had the dog tried to chase her than the townspeople had thrown stones at it, and it had to turn away. Tonight it had happened upon a better form of entertainment. It hung out its tongue, gulped and began to bark with ferocity.

Limping from the knock against the flowerpot, the corporal ran. The moonless night did not offer him many choices in his escape route. He ran until he reached a dead end, at which point he turned round and, feeling about, tried to discover another way. A moment later he splashed across a ditch. His nose told him it was the sewer: he was entering the slum. As a final act of despair, he dropped his boots in the conduit before plunging into the filth.

He swore at his bad luck, but not for an instant did he regret his decision to desert. The apparition of his female correspondent flashed in his eyes. He had never received a photograph from her despite his pleas, but he had fashioned her face from her handwriting as well as an artist's rendition of an Egyptian queen, a crumpled newspaper clipping he kept in his wallet: black straight hair, almond-shaped eyes, strong long nose, stubborn lips.

What his pleading and curses had failed to achieve was suddenly achieved by the sound of a whistle. The dog stopped, pricked up its ears and wagged its tail. It had alerted the patrol. It could hear them at this moment, still far away, rushing. It barked again to direct them towards the runaway. It was not long before their lanterns shone at the other end of the alleyway.

'Halt!'

The corporal did not stop. There were shots in the air, and the guards scrambled to arrest him, shouting to each other over the walls to coordinate their search. But it was difficult, even with their lanterns and the help of the dog. The maze generated a confusion of echoes and shadows that led the soldiers astray and caused exchanges of friendly fire. There were no casualties, but more time was lost, while the corporal went deeper into the slum. By now his socks were torn and his feet were bleeding, but somehow he had managed to shake off the soldiers and the dog. Separated from the rest of the town by the open sewer, the houses of the slum were made out of wood, tin and tarpaulin. When the corporal stopped and spun round, looking for an exit, faces peered at him from windows without panes. A hand stretched out and offered him a lit lantern. He took it and was about to thank his saviour when the noise of the patrol made his panic return.

The pursuit resumed. With the help of the light, the corporal came out a few minutes later from the labyrinth. A bullet cut short his joy. It bored through the flesh of his arm and went on to smash his lamp to pieces. Against the dark sky, the corporal saw the huge dome of Saint Gregorius Theologus. A flickering light was coming from its nave, and the corporal remembered that the padre had moved in there. He thought, 'I'm saved.'

It was a beautiful dream, the kind he had not dreamed for years. He was still in town, but instead of his army uniform he wore his cassock. Time had passed – he could not exactly tell how long – and there had been changes. There was no slum any more, but modest stone houses with pleasant gardens. A small park stood where the *hamam* used to be.

Madame Violetta's villa had been converted into a school where girls were taught home economics. The open sewer had been covered, and the smell that dominated the town was finally gone. It was all the result of Father Simeon's efforts. In his dream he was ringing the bells, and a crowd of pious converts were flocking to the restored church.

There was also something strange about his dream. Wherever he went he carried on his shoulder a crow. The way Father Simeon understood it, it must have symbolised his guilt for not having achieved the clerical ambition of his youth of becoming a missionary. But he had redeemed himself at last, and *there* was now the proof in his dream: the crow opened its wings and flew off his shoulder. Father Simeon, Apostle of All Anatolians, contemplated it with tranquil eyes.

There was a knock on the door. The padre barely noticed the sound in his sleep. The crow in his dream flew above the dome of Saint Gregorius Theologus, letting out little shrieks. There was a second hammering on the door, but again Father Simeon refused to abandon his dream. Where was he? Oh yes, the crow of his guilt. There it was, flying away, soon to disappear for ever. Suddenly the bird turned round and came back, perching again on the priest's shoulder. Father Simeon began to weep in his sleep. There was another knock on the door. This time the padre had fewer reasons not to wake up.

'Go away!' he shouted and pulled his coat over his head.

The thumping continued. Finally he stood up and threw his coat over his shoulders. He went to the narthex, removed the piece of wood that propped the door shut and opened. On the steps of the church stood the corporal. Father Simeon rubbed his eyes.

'If you've come for a confession, my son,' he yawned, 'say two Our Fathers before going to bed and one more first thing in the morning. Then come and see me.'

The corporal staggered back and forth on the church steps.

He appeared not to have his boots on. The padre looked closer and saw that the corporal was wearing only his socks, which were in tatters.

'What's all this?' he asked.

'Let me in, Father.'

Only then did the padre notice that the corporal's arm was bleeding.

'You need medical assistance,' he said. 'I've nothing here.'

'Father, you have to hide me.'

'Cotton . . . dressings . . . carbolic . . .' mumbled the padre.

A whistle sounded somewhere, and the corporal turned his head and listened. His pursuers were still in the alleyways of the slum.

'*Please*, Father.'

Father Simeon put his hands in his pockets. He was wide awake now. His instinct had always been to help the needy.

'But this could be serious,' he said. 'In the infirmary you'll find—'

The young soldier looked at his wound and tried to smile.

'This? Nothing to worry about. I get cut deeper when I'm shaving.'

He wiped the sweat from his forehead with the hand that had been pressing his wound and smeared his face with blood. The padre was reminded of the face of Jesus on the cross.

'Please, Father,' the corporal repeated.

Another of the padre's instincts was to comply with the law, even though there had been certain exceptions lately. The situation on the steps of the church concerned a true and unmitigated crime: desertion.

Father Simeon said, 'I'm the moral compass of . . . Any decision that would . . .'

He thought about the items he had stolen from the brigadier's quarters that night and which were inside the church at that moment. What if the patrol were to search the place? The risk was too high.

130

'Impossible,' he said. 'It would be a crime . . . And I an accessory.'

A cold wind blew past him and entered the church through the half-opened door. The fire on the floor of the nave flickered. Sparks shone in the corporal's eyes. The padre looked down.

'I'm afraid there is nothing I can do for you,' he said.

There was shouting in the slum, and the dog began to bark again. The padre recognised Caleb's voice.

'I advise you to give yourself up,' he said. 'Where would you go in your condition?'

The corporal glanced at his arm as if it were something he had picked up in the street. His sleeve was soaked in blood.

'I'm a deserter, Father.'

In the distance the argument ended. Only the barking of the dog could be heard, coming closer.

'Even if I helped you there is nothing out there,' the padre said. 'It wouldn't be long before the jackals—'

'I stand more chance against the jackals than the firing squad, Father.'

'I promise to speak to the brigadier. He's a reasonable man. It's a miracle the circumstances haven't driven him insane.'

The young man felt a numbness spread down his arm. He was tired; all this was not meant to happen.

'I only wanted to go home, Father.'

The padre tried to smile but managed a caricature of his intended expression.

'Home. Of course. You're young. Our country needs you. After the war it'll be men like you . . .'

'I beg you, Father.'

A slight sense of impatience came over the priest.

'Yes, yes. I'll do everything in my power to help.'

Caleb appeared at the end of the street. He lifted his leg, sniffed the air and recognised his master. Father Simeon placed his hand on the young man's shoulder.

131

'The risk is great. My position . . . delicate. You understand?'

The dog came towards them, wagging its tail. At both ends of the street lanterns swung in the dark.

'Mother,' the corporal said. 'Oh, mother.'

Father Simeon bit his lip.

'Ask the Lord for forgiveness. Only He—'

The corporal rushed down the steps of the church in a last attempt to escape. But he was surrounded. He knelt down and remained silent. Someone had found his backpack. He emptied it in the middle of the street and searched through it. He picked up the communist pamphlet and put it in his pocket. Then he tied up the corporal, saluted the padre and took the deserter away.

Not far away Major Porfirio lay on his cot. The commotion had awakened him. When he heard the patrol pass under his window, he immediately guessed what had happened. 'Fool,' he said. 'The end was so near. One way or another.' He blew out the lamp and stayed in the dark with his eyes open.

A small candle stuck in the neck of a bottle lit the interior of the shack, a single room without partitions. The floor was laid with clay. The furnishings, old and discarded objects repaired with patience, gave the impression of sick animals that had crawled in there to die. In a corner was a large piece of earthenware filled with water: the sink. Elsewhere, a string of onions hung from the rafters. A mattress was placed directly on the floor; a rough blanket covered the couple but offered little protection from the cold. Annina pulled the blanket over her neck.

'You'll tell me when it's time, yes?' she said. 'I don't want Madame to wake up and find I'm missing.'

Yusuf tucked her up and ran a pair of fingers over the blanket.

'Don't worry. The rats tell the time better than a Swiss clock. In the morning they always go back to the church.'

The maid could not stop the rattling of her teeth.

132

'I'm a little cold tonight,' she said.

Yusuf rose slowly from the bed.

'Why didn't you say so? I'll fetch the hot-water bottle.'

He found the spirit stove and boiled some water. Then he took the pot and disappeared into a dark corner of the shack. He returned to bed with a rubber inner tube.

'In a minute the bed will be as hot as Hell,' he said.

Annina shivered.

'Don't say that on a night like this. It makes me scared.'

Yusuf arranged the inner tube under the covers before getting into bed again.

'Why? You have nothing to worry about. You'll go to Paradise. Hell is for the rich.'

'I'm thinking of that soldier.'

Yusuf shook his head.

'Yes. He may go to Paradise or maybe to Hell. God will decide.'

That night's incident had excited them both. They could not go back to sleep.

'It was so noble of you to give him the lamp,' Annina said. She took her hand out of the covers and stroked her lover's face. 'My kind Yusuf.'

The Arab kissed her fingers.

'But we have no light now,' he said modestly. 'And he's in prison all the same.'

'He must be very desperate to try such a thing.'

'A fool, more likely. He stood no chance.'

'Only a man in love could be so desperate,' insisted the Frenchwoman.

They were like two people looking at a piece of embroidery from opposite sides: she was impressed by the romanticism of the man's impulse, but all the Arab could see were loose threads and ugly knots.

'Not a chance,' Yusuf repeated. 'There're wolves out there. And brigands. Without a map? Impossible.'

'The call of love lured him like the Sirens,' Annina said.

The Arab was familiar with the ancient myth.

'Then he should've plugged his ears.'

He had met Annina at the end of a long journey that in retrospect seemed like a pilgrimage with some exalted purpose. He had left his home, a small village in the land of the Nubians, in search of work. He was only ten when he had found his first job, carrying rubble at the site of the first Aswan dam. At twelve he was already working in a quarry, splitting granite from dawn until he could no longer see the steamboats on the river. He often talked to Annina about his home with yearning and adulation. 'The best place in the world,' he would say. 'The houses swim in the sacred Nile. One day I'll take you there.' Less than forty years later, in the dusk of his life, construction of a bigger dam would start at Aswan, and an enormous artificial lake would submerge his birthplace.

He would still be living there had he not been struck down by tuberculosis before his sixteenth birthday. When the disease had gone away two years later, he was left with a hunched back and contorted ribs, which made it difficult for him to breathe: he could work in the quarry no more. For a long time, he wandered across the Levant, doing menial jobs: street sweeper, bootblack, tool sharpener. What drove him to travel was not a desire to know foreign lands but the embarrassment caused by his deformity. After a few weeks in a place, when the people started recognising him in the street, he would become convinced that their stare was directed towards the weight he carried on his shoulders: they were all fascinated by his hump. He had once walked into a butcher's and demanded that he operate on his back with the cleaver, but the butcher had refused.

He had finally found refuge from the world in a remote *madrasa*, where he was apprenticed to its nonagenarian gardener and his melancholy macaque, the only beings not to notice his crooked back, unaware that his patron was blind

134

and the monkey had enough troubles of its own. With the old man's help, Yusuf discovered his vocation in life and shed his bashfulness. In a visit to the nearby town, he had met Annina. She had fallen in love with him at first sight because at the time she had been reading *Notre Dame of Paris* and had been moved by the character of the tortured hunchback Quasimodo.

Under the covers Yusuf searched with his toes for the hot inner tube.

'The sea is for fish, the desert is for camel and the road is for man,' he said. 'That soldier had to be patient.'

'You've crossed deserts yourself, haven't you?'

The Arab smiled in the dark.

'But I'm a camel. Can't you see the hump?'

'Your life reminds me of a book,' Annina said tenderly. 'I think it was called *The Life and Adventures of Robinson . . . Croesus.*'

'I know him. King, yes?'

'No. He was a sailor.'

The man shrugged his shoulders.

'Then I don't know him. The sea takes many men every day.'

'It's the true story of a brave man. I wish I could've met him. What stories he would have to tell.'

The Arab felt a pang of jealousy.

'Enough,' he said. 'It'll be dawn soon. Better sleep a little.'

He had already fallen asleep when a moment later Annina tapped him on the shoulder.

'Yusuf?'

'Mm.'

'I think we ought to pray for that soldier.'

Yusuf yawned and shook his head submissively. They began to pray quietly, each in their own tongue and to their own god, until their exhaustion silenced them both and ordered them to sleep.

135

13

The following morning the town awakened to a torrential rainstorm. While the people slept, a wind began to blow from the sea, foretelling the storm. In a steady stream of salty air, the wind brought to the town seashells, sponges and starfish, a strange hail that lasted until the roofs began to resemble the ocean floor. The crows hid under the eaves, and soon the rain started, building up strength fast. After the lashing of the wind, the rain stripped the tamarisks of their last leaves. Tiles slipped off roofs, drainpipes clogged, flower beds were swallowed by the mud. The rain flooded the open sewer and turned the slum into a swamp, forcing the people to flee their shacks and find refuge on the higher ground of the town square where, barefoot, they stood shivering, waiting for the storm to pass. From a window on the top floor of the Town Hall, the medic watched the silent figures soak in the rain.

'By the end of the month,' he said, 'several will have died of pneumonia.'

He returned to his work. In the middle of the room, the corporal sat on a chair with his hands tied behind his back and his feet chained. A battered metal box with a faded red cross was on the table. The medic cut his patient's sleeve with a pair of scissors. Blood and pus had clotted on the skin. Having cleaned the injury, the medic held the arm gently and studied the damage caused by the bullet with a magnifying glass.

'Entry point,' he said and looked on the other side. 'Penetrating. Some damage to the triceps.' He shook his head.

'You're even less of an escape artist than a chess player, corporal.' He searched through his medical box. 'This'll sting a little.'

He poured antiseptic over the wound and watched the acid burn through the tissue. The pain brought the corporal back from his stupor.

'Bastard,' he said with clenched teeth. 'You'll never forgive me for the time I forced a draw on you.'

The medic poured more antiseptic over the wound. The corporal cried again.

'It's a well-known fact that the English Opening is for cowards,' the medic said. 'Every other game ends in a draw.'

The rain thumped the window. Water crept in over the sill. A soldier with a small head and the expression of a ruminating animal sat on a stool by the door with his rifle propped against the wall.

'This man has to be taken to the infirmary,' the medic said.

'Out of the question,' the guard said.

'At least untie his hands. He has to be operated on.'

The soldier again shook his head.

'The brigadier has given strict orders.'

'I can't treat him like that. Unless you want him to die of gangrene.'

'As long as it happens on that chair. He deserves whatever he gets.'

The rain subsided briefly, and the wind began. Tiles slipped off the roof of the Town Hall and crashed to the courtyard with the marble bust.

'Medic,' the corporal said, 'I want you to read me something. Look in my pocket.'

The medic searched the tunic, but the love letters were nowhere to be found.

'All documents have been passed on to the brigadier,' the guard said. 'He's personally in charge of the investigation.'

The medic soaked a pad of gauze in chloroform.

'If you did all that for the love of a woman I'd do better to operate on your brain.'

The corporal did not laugh.

'Love can achieve everything.'

'It won't deflect a bullet,' the medic said.

He placed the pad with the anaesthetic over his patient's face. The corporal fell asleep, but the medic did not remove the pad from his face. The chloroform was enough to cause cardiac paralysis: for a moment the medic thought that he would be doing his patient a service if he made sure he never woke up again. Reminding himself of the Hippocratic oath, he threw away the pad with the anaesthetic and removed the lid of the canister with the sterilised tools.

In the church the padre was dressing. He was still shaken by the events of the previous night. He had stayed awake, trying to justify to himself his decision to refuse the runaway shelter. He had failed. The wind broke against the walls of the church like waves on a rock. He tied the laces of his boots and began to wind his puttees around his legs.

'But he had committed a crime,' he said. 'According to army rules.'

He was not used to questioning his faith. He thought that the Lord ought to know by then that every decision he, the padre, made in his life was intended to confirm His glory. Having finished with the puttees, he slung his braces over his shoulders. It had started to rain again.

'It wasn't myself I was thinking of last night,' he said. 'No, Lord. It was *You*.'

The wind whistled through the broken windows. Father Simeon covered his ears with his hands.

'This wind,' he said. 'It sounds like the trumpets of Jericho.'

Somewhere inside the church the dog was chasing rats, but they were too fast for him. Caleb stuck his muzzle in a hole in the wall. Contemplating his companion, the padre buttoned up his shirt. There was nowhere to hang his clothes, and his tunic, like the rest of his uniform, lay on the floor. He picked it up and beat it with his hand; a cloud of dust made him sneeze.

'My life I handed over to You,' he continued. 'Body and soul. See this glass eye? For Your glory, too.'

The weather worsened his melancholy. The stones of Saint Gregorius Theologus stopped the rain, but a cold wind continued to blow through the broken windows. The fire in the nave had burned out. Father Simeon shivered. His tunic offered little protection.

'The temptations are always so many. When one is surrounded by . . . *You* should understand. There's always a Mary Magdalene to anoint one's feet.'

Even at his age and with his eye injury, the evidence was there to support his argument. He had been not only the spiritual leader of his village but also the most handsome among the male members of his parish. There had been numerous occasions . . . He stopped and raised a finger.

'But *I* never succumbed,' he said.

The ingeniousness of his faith was that it led to happiness through the denial of pleasure – and, even, through the espousal of pain. Father Simeon recalled how as a young cleric he used to practise self-flagellation, a crude but efficient way to purge his mind of sin. It was a very long time ago, of course. Since then he had developed the mental abilities to stop the darkness before it entered his mind.

'All I want is to spread Your word to these heathens. And I need the Gospel to do it.'

Caleb yelped and pulled his muzzle out of the hole in the wall. The sound travelled across the nave, entered the narthex and a moment later was heard coming from the opposite end of the church. Attracted to the echo, the dog abandoned its game and walked towards the altar, expecting to find another dog there.

'I need the bible and the church and the icons,' Father Simeon said. 'And I need the wine for the communion and the oil and the candles.'

He raised his eye to the mural high above his head. The dome sat on an array of windows whose circle of light, even on such an overcast morning, made the austere face of the Pantocrator seem poised in mid-air.

'For what is faith without the power and the glory?' the padre asked.

He put on his greatcoat and his kepi. The weather did not seem to be easing. Father Simeon was glad: it meant there would be fewer soldiers in the streets. He hushed the dog with a single word, cupped his hand behind his ear and listened. Satisfied there was no one else in the building, he knelt down and lifted one of the heavy tiles. In a hole in the floor, wrapped in cloth, were Brigadier Nestor's ceremonial sword and riding boots with the silver spurs. He could not resist untying the string and having a quick glance. The shine of the polished metal and the expensive leather lit up his tired face: the precious Gospel would soon be his.

'Do you know who Zephyrus was?'

The orderly shrugged his shoulders. Brigadier Nestor nodded with disappointment.

'It's a pity when one doesn't know one's history,' he said. 'But it's almost a crime to be ignorant of one's mythology.'

His orderly continued to polish his commanding officer's belt and holster.

'Because mythology is more than history, son. It's also science. Like, for example, the west wind blasting us all morning. Our ancestors would say that Zephyrus was responsible for it. The son of a Titan and the goddess of the dawn. Also, he was married to Iris, goddess of the rainbow.'

Brigadier Nestor looked out: more clouds were gathering above the town. He pursed his lips.

'His brothers were Boreas and Notus,' he continued. 'The gods of the north and south winds respectively.'

The boy nodded mechanically. He finished the polishing and began cleaning his superior's revolver. A long time had gone by, but he still remembered the time when one of the mules of the baggage train had thrown itself into a ditch and snapped its leg. Brigadier Nestor's lorry had happened to be passing by, and the old man had witnessed the incident. He had given the boy his pistol and ordered him to take care of the matter. His hand had shaken when he rested the muzzle on the animal's forehead. The idiot's eyes of the mule, its enormous teeth, its desperate braying: it had been the only time the orderly had killed a living being.

The brigadier continued to pace the room.

'Zephyrus was also a courier of the gods,' he said. 'If our ancestors were here today they'd reason that this wind out there carries a divine message.'

A bolt of lightning struck the rod on the roof and made the windows shake. The orderly cowered. The electric discharge seemed to rip open the sky, and a heavy downpour started. Brigadier Nestor raised his eyes to the ceiling.

'This particular message probably says the gods aren't happy with the situation,' he said.

His orderly had worked hard to transform the conference room into his superior's quarters. The dustsheets had been removed, and the furniture had been polished. The floor had been mopped and waxed, the nails that stood up from the boards had been hammered back in, carpets had been brought from other rooms.

'And neither am *I* happy,' the brigadier added, getting tired. 'Any news?'

He was waiting for the return of Major Porfirio, who had been put in charge of the search for his boots and sword. Water dripped from the ceiling into pots placed across the room. The stolen items had always been of sentimental

141

importance to the old officer. He had been presented with them at his graduation from the Military Academy, one of the happiest days of his life.

'The year was 1881,' he said in a melancholy voice. 'I was your age. Twenty-one.'

At the graduation ceremony, he had shaken the hands of his tutors, saluted the generals attending, kissed the hem of the flag and delivered a valedictory speech that had roused his fellow graduates. Just one look at his graduation uniform had always been enough to remind him of that afternoon more than forty years before.

'Our dog ate the aigrette only a few months later,' he said. 'Then, one year, I forgot to spread camphor in the wardrobe, and the moths drilled into the tunic and trousers. In the autumn I gave them to our gardener to dress the scarecrow.'

The young soldier finished his task. Brigadier Nestor put on his belt, picked up his revolver and placed its muzzle to his temple.

'If I'm not mistaken,' he said, 'the last time this pistol was used was to shoot a mule, yes? Sometimes I feel it'll be next used for a similar reason.'

He squeezed the trigger. The empty cylinder turned, and the hammer hit with a dull sound.

'Yes, very likely,' the old man said and searched for the bullets.

By the time he placed the loaded pistol in its holster, he was feeling better. On the edge of the conference table lay the communist pamphlet found on the corporal. The brigadier riffled through it.

'So. If it weren't for Cerberus, the Bolshevik would have slipped away from right under our noses.'

'Caleb, my brigadier.'

Brigadier Nestor nodded.

'That canine deserves a decoration for extreme vigilance.'

The rain continued but with less intensity. The brigadier walked up to the window and stood watching the rain with his hands clasped behind his back. Heavy clouds still hovered over the roofs. Beyond the limits of the town the sky had already cleared, and the sun was drying the hills. The old man dropped into an armchair.

'We've stayed here too long,' he said.

In actual fact they had arrived in the town only a few days earlier. The repairs were almost finished, the animals had rested, and enough provisions had been requisitioned to last the final march to the sea. The brigade was going to be on its way soon. The orderly left the room, only to return a minute later and inform his superior that the air lieutenant was there to see him. Brigadier Nestor remembered their appointment.

'Ah yes,' he said. 'Give me a moment.'

His orderly left. It was time for his dose. That morning, without even getting out of bed, he had reached for the cigar box under his cot and filled the syringe. Over the past few days, his craving for the drug had increased. The quantity he needed to hold on to his sanity doubled every other day, and the frequency of the injections tripled. But even so, at night his mind would always travel back to the massacre, and the memory of the event came to him more and more vividly. His fascination with classical mythology made him dream of the Furies too. Every night the three avenging deities would ascend from the underworld to pursue him without mercy, their wings flapping, the snakes in their hair writhing, their eyes dripping blood.

By now he had given up sterilising the needle over the flame. He pulled it from his vein and sat back in his armchair. He let the empty syringe slip out of his hand and watched it roll away on the floor. Outside, the rain still menaced the town. Under his skin the drug galloped. He recalled the seance he had attended the previous evening. What had the Armenian woman said? *Some vultures circle above your head; others walk alongside you.*

'That witch was right,' he said.

He stayed in the armchair still and exhausted for what seemed like a great length of time. When he turned his eyes to the clock on the wall, he discovered that only five minutes had passed. He waited until the drug began to work. Then he shouted in the direction of the door. Promptly the airman entered.

'Come, lieutenant. I'm afraid I have very little time. An interrogation to take care of. I guess you've heard.'

The young officer saluted and removed his cap.

'The arrest, yes.'

Brigadier Nestor remained seated.

'Indeed. It was about time I cleaned my bed of ticks.'

'Your bed?'

'The brigade, son. Of criminal elements.'

'Ah. That's exactly the reason I've come to see you, sir. The . . . extermination of ticks.'

Brigadier Nestor was getting excited.

'The atheist Bolshevik attempting to hide in the church. How's that for an irony?'

Air Lieutenant Kimon was anxious now to share his knowledge.

'Divine justice, brigadier. Divine justice.'

'Yes. Because the padre is a buttress against corruption,' the senior officer said. 'Sometimes, I admit, he gets on my nerves, but overall he's an indispensable part of this unit. Both he and the dog.'

'Caleb?'

'Cerberus,' the brigadier said. 'He smelt the Bolshevik from a mile away. What was it that you wanted to see me about?'

'I may have a piece of information that could be of relevance to the case.'

Brigadier Nestor raised his eyebrows.

'Relevance? Right. Enlighten me then, lieutenant.'

The airman revealed everything he knew about Major Porfirio and the release of the horse. When he finished he felt a sense of relief. There was a jug of water on the conference table. After being granted permission, he filled a glass from it and drank.

'Porfirio?' Brigadier Nestor asked. 'An officer of his abilities? Impossible.'

'I saw him free the horse with my own eyes, brigadier. And, if you remember, later the same night someone filled the camp with handbills.'

'But surely you can't be certain. The rainstorm, the night . . .'

'Oh, it was him.'

Brigadier Nestor twisted the tip of his moustache. The morphia had dulled his brain. He remembered another of the medium's warnings: *A plain tunic conceals the truth well; one with insignia does it better.*

'I must be senile not to have seen it,' he said.

The frequent appearances of the handbills, the thefts, the absence of witnesses: being his Chief of Staff, the major could have done all this without being suspected – and the diversion he had created by claiming that his own wine and razor had been stolen. It was clever. Brigadier Nestor had solved the mystery. After such a long time, he would have expected to feel triumphant. Instead he felt a strange sense of loss. He called his orderly.

'Send the patrol to arrest Porfirio,' he said gloomily. 'And search his quarters inch by inch.'

The rain eased a little, and the wind died away. The clouds stood over the town, laden and quiet. The muddy streets filled with people. The stench of the flooded sewer covered the smells of the market. The calm did not last. Mr Othon was on his way to the *hamam* when the rain started again. The crowd scattered. The schoolmaster found shelter under the awning

145

of the grocery. Leaning on his broom, the Armenian watched the rain from the door of his shop.

'If this carries on a little longer, only an ark will save us,' he said.

The schoolmaster wrung out his hat.

'This is the worst autumn in living memory. And the storm isn't over yet. When I left home, the barometer was still falling.'

The grocer crossed himself.

'Maybe the Adventists are right, after all.'

During the Great War, an American pastor had stayed briefly in town on his way to Mesopotamia. He was a young man of worldly elegance and so much wisdom that the schoolmaster had regarded it as arrogance. The pastor had told the people that he was an amateur archaeologist whose aim was to discover the Tower of Babel but spent more time preaching the tenets of his faith than planning his search. He believed in the Second Coming of the Lord Jesus Christ, which he insisted was imminent, and in the observance of Saturday as the Sabbath. When one evening the townspeople had invited him to a dance, he had looked at them disapprovingly and said that that was an activity second in wickedness only to theatre-going. Another time he had explained to the schoolmaster how the human body was the temple of the Holy Ghost and therefore one should refrain from eating meat and smoking tobacco.

'I still believe he was a spy of the Allied Powers,' Mr Othon said.

He sat on the bench outside the grocery and began to knead his crumpled hat back into shape. It had been a birthday present from Violetta.

'Have you talked to the mayor yet?' the grocer asked.

'The Beau Brummell of Anatolia,' Mr Othon hissed. 'The hell with him.'

The grocer looked at the rain streaming down the awning.

The street was a swamp where pallets, barrels and cartwheels floated past. Further up on the opposite side, someone was trying to find a crossing. The rain kept coming down, and the street was turning into a faster torrent, flowing towards the town square. Suddenly the man plunged into the current. What he thought was a shoal was in fact a floating plank, and he began to sink in the mud. 'Help!' he cried and struggled to stay on the surface. He grabbed the plank that had lured him in, but he had to let it go after a moment because it was dragging him away. The Armenian rushed to the steps of his shop and held out his broom. The drowning man managed to swim a few feet and reach the broomstick. The grocer and the schoolmaster helped him out of the mud and sat him on the veranda of the grocery. It was not until he wiped the mud off his face that they recognised him.

'Thank you,' the padre said.

'You almost had the honour of being the first man to drown this year,' the schoolmaster said.

The padre was shivering. The Armenian offered him a brandy and returned inside the shop to inspect the leaks in the roof.

'*By the breath of God frost is given*,' the padre said. 'There's nothing one can do.'

'One day man will be able to change the weather at will,' the schoolmaster said.

'Impossible. The skies are the realm of the Lord.'

'There've already been experiments of limited success. Dynamite attached to balloons has been detonated in the clouds to induce precipitation.'

Father Simeon gave him a sidelong glance.

'You sound like a heretic.'

'I'm a scientist, Father.'

The padre puffed. Even in that desolate place that God threatened to abandon, science had crawled in. He wanted to leave the shelter, but the torrent stopped him.

147

'You aren't going to tell me that you believe the theories of that German too?' he asked.

Mr Othon moved a little on the bench to avoid a drip from the awning.

'German? You mean Einstein? I would if I could understand them myself. He's without a doubt the greatest scientist since Newton. Perhaps even greater than him.'

'Newton was an enlightened Christian, not a mystical Semite.'

Father Simeon waved at a raft with armed soldiers passing in front of the grocery. They agreed to put him down on the first bit of dry land.

It took him a long time to reach home. By midday the whole town seemed to be sinking into the swamp that overflowed with litter, drowned animals and the excrement of the open sewer. When he finally climbed the steps of Saint Gregorius Theologus, he was exhausted and wet to the bone. As soon as he opened the door, he was confronted with a horrible sight: the rain had flooded the crypt of the church, and the floor was carpeted with the corpses of rats. Quietly, he closed the door again and squeezed himself under the eaves outside. Protected from the rain, he unbuttoned his tunic. The parcel was wrapped in several layers of canvas, which he began to remove with emotion. After a few wet layers, the rest were dry. Holding the medieval Gospel close to his heart, he waited for the storm to pass. It should not be long: beyond the town the weather had already cleared, and a faint rainbow was running across the sky.

14

Between the creaking of the bed, she heard the chirping of the birds bathing in the cistern out in the garden. She moved her eyes across the walls, where a row of tall windows lit the room. From where she lay, she saw things she had not noticed until then: chinks in the wooden floor, holes in the drapery, green rust on the door hinges. It was not until she raised her eyes to the ceiling that her curiosity turned into sadness: the slow crumbling of the stucco relief had also gone unnoticed for quite some time.

The house was decorated heavily: the spiral staircase with the carved handrail, the marble floor in the downstairs living room, the fountain with urinating cherubs in the garden. She studied the gypsum decorations on the ceiling. Under layers of cobweb were acanthus leaves, birds with broken beaks, headless snakes, monkeys whose tails had fallen off. She felt as if she were not in her bedroom but a public place. For the first time in her life, Violetta questioned the purpose of her situation.

The bed continued to creak rhythmically. Every time the headboard hit the wall, it brought down a piece of plaster. For a while Violetta listened to the noise.

'What a pity this house ended up like this,' she said. 'It's even grander than your church.'

'Huh?'

The mayor paused and wiped the sweat off his forehead. He was wearing only his vest and his socks. He searched among his clothes, which were scattered over the floor, until he found the copy of the Kama Sutra. He studied the illustrations.

'I don't understand,' he said and turned the book upside down. 'This is humanly impossible.'

'Let me see.'

Violetta read the text that accompanied the illustrations.

'Oh, it's a bad translation,' she said.

'No one reads it for its literary value,' the mayor said.

'One has to be fit.'

The mayor pouted.

'No. A contortionist.'

He gave up and lay next to his lover. He had come across the book in the municipal library during one of his periodic attempts to clean up the room and had immediately signed it out on permanent loan to himself. Every time he paid Violetta a visit, he brought it along.

'What did you say about the church?' the mayor asked.

Violetta repeated her comment.

'That church is a rat-hole,' the mayor replied.

Soaked in sweat his vest stuck to his chest. He took in deep breaths. The birds chirped in the garden.

'How come I never see a rat in *your* house?' he asked.

'Yusuf brings the cat over a couple of times a week,' the woman let slip.

The mayor hit his fist on the bed.

'Damn Turk. That cat is municipal property. If there was law in this town, I'd have him arrested for embezzlement.'

The woman rolled her head on her pillow and looked outside. The breeze lifted the curtains off the floor. Violetta thought of the sea. She had not been to the coast for years. When she lived in France, she used to spend summers on the Côte d'Azur, where she swam a mile every morning before breakfast. Next to her the mayor was still talking about the cat.

'Any private user should first lodge an application with the office of sanitation and pay the appropriate fee.'

Violetta's silk kimono was on its hanger next to the bed. She stretched out her arm and reached it, put it on and propped herself up on the pillows.

'The office of sanitation is the closet where you keep the mop and bucket,' she said, tying the ribbon of the robe about her waist.

The mayor grunted in reply. Bathed in sweat as he was, the breeze made him shiver. But he knew his lover liked to keep the windows open, and he did not complain. He fingered the ribbon of her kimono.

'Anyway. Have I told you the story of this?' he asked amorously.

The kimono was among the spoils of a game of poker, which had begun on an evening years before in a hotel in Izmir and had lasted twenty-one hours. The final round had been between the mayor and the captain of a merchant ship that had just arrived from the Far East. The captain was a bearded giant with cardinal cheeks, a sexual passion for card games and more mettle than actual wealth. A cabin boy he had brought along to serve him drinks had soon been ordered to carry over from the ship anything that could be bet on the game. Soon the treasures were piled up both on the table and the floor, among them the kimono and the ship's gyro-compass. The instrument had been an unwise stake: a week after the game, the ship had hit shoals in the Red Sea and sunk. All the crew had managed to abandon ship apart from the captain, who had gone down with it, cursing the mayor, who had won the game of poker.

Violetta sighed. The retelling of the story bored her. Besides, there was something else on her mind.

'What will they do to that man?' she asked.

'You mean the deserter?'

'Yes.'

'In fact it's two men now,' the mayor said. 'They arrested the major yesterday, too. I used to think of him as a nice fellow, but he turned out to be a conspirator. It goes to show that you can trust no one these days.'

His watch was on the bedside table. He opened its cover and read the time.

'I have to go. Nothing in this town moves without me pushing it.' Then he noted his lover's anxiety. 'Don't worry, my dear. The brigadier is a reasonable man. Those men have suffered enough, what with the fighting and the retreat.'

He gathered his clothes from the floor and put them on, whistling.

'Can one see them?' Violetta asked.

Her lover frowned.

'I don't think they'd have the time to receive visitors. They should be occupied with the interrogation.'

'Will they be treated badly?'

The mayor began to whistle again. Looking in the mirror of the dressing table, he tied his tie.

'Well, I have no doubt the brigadier will use his full powers of persuasion,' he said. He buttoned up his shirt and contemplated his reflection. 'I need a new collar.'

Violetta put her arm under her head.

'Send the shirt over. Annina will do it for you.'

The sun hid behind the clouds, leaving behind the memory of summer. The mayor sat on the edge of the bed to tie up his laces.

'Maybe I should take them some food,' the woman said.

'Whom?'

'The prisoners.'

The mayor went back to tying his laces.

'You? Oh, I'm sure they're well looked after.'

She did not reply. He turned and touched the little bit of her shoulder that emerged from the covers.

'Listen,' he said. 'We're civilians. We're not supposed to get involved. Even I have no authority over—'

A bird came in at one window. Violetta put her finger to her lips and hushed her fiancé. He gave the bird an indifferent look before hooking the chain of his watch on his waistcoat and putting on his hat. Having chirped a few notes, the bird flew off the sill again.

'*Jolie*,' Violetta said. '*Que fais tu dans ce désert?*'

The mayor thought he understood.

'Mm? I love you too. Very much. But I do have to go. Duty calls.'

He kissed her on the forehead and left. In the bedroom, Violetta sat alone, thinking about the major and the corporal.

The major's quarters were in an attic with a low ceiling and a single window. He had arranged his cot so that the light of dawn would wake him as soon as the sun rose above the hills. The soldiers who searched the place found neither the sword nor the pair of boots with the silver spurs but noticed a pair of loose floorboards. When they lifted them, they discovered the crate with Major Porfirio's books and the ancient mimeograph he used to print the handbills. They were still examining what they had discovered when the door opened and the major walked in. Calmly he raised his arms, no sign of surprise in his eyes.

In the Town Hall, Brigadier Nestor paced round the conference table, waiting for the soldiers to return. Now and again he stopped to check his watch, but his eyes did not register the time. The recent events had affected him as much as the defeat. He did not care for the corporal; a deserter was a coward whether the army was in retreat or not – it was discipline that had kept them alive so far. And, let them not forget, they were not safe yet; the enemy could still be after them. It was imperative that he make an example of the corporal. The floor creaked under his boots.

He thought differently of his Chief of Staff. 'Damn you,

153

Porfirio,' he said. 'The last thing I needed was your ghost hovering over my grave.' He felt nauseous and had to grab the table to steady himself. As he leaned over, his morning coffee poured out of his mouth. He pulled up a chair and sat down. He had decided to quit morphia. He suffered from diarrhoea, sleeplessness and fever. And then there was the pain: his bones, his muscles, his abdomen. It was not the first time he had wanted to quit. The medic had warned him that it would be difficult. It had proved impossible. He thought, a few more days, until we reach the coast. Then I'll give it up. He shouted through the closed door that he did not wish to be disturbed, then walked to his trunk, where he hid the tools of his torment.

Some time later he opened his eyes and looked out of the window. A group of soldiers was crossing the square in a brisk manner. Walking among them, with his hands tied behind his back, was his Chief of Staff. There was a knock on the door.

'I said, I don't want to be disturbed.'

From the other side of the door, his orderly told him that the major had been arrested and evidence had been seized. Brigadier Nestor hid the syringe, checked his appearance in the mirror and asked him to bring it in. His orderly set the crate with the books and the mimeograph on the floor. Before leaving, the boy noticed the vomit.

'Are you well, my brigadier?'

'What? Oh, I'm fine. That coffee made my stomach turn. Clean it up, please.'

His orderly returned with the mop and bucket. While he cleaned the vomit, there was a knock on the door. The old man puffed.

'What now?'

He recognised the war correspondent's voice and groaned.

'Come in, friend,' he called.

The journalist entered, rubbing his hands with exhilaration.

154

'Dramatic developments, my brigadier. What more could we have asked for, eh?'

Brigadier Nestor frowned.

'Salvation?'

'Oh it'll come. You're as good as saved. Only a matter of time.'

'A matter of time. Indeed.'

'Yes. In the meantime, the two conspirators will add the necessary intrigue to my articles. I've started to write already.'

The orderly picked up the mop and bucket and left the room. The war correspondent glanced in it.

'My brigadier? Are you well?'

Brigadier Nestor rubbed his eyes.

'Why is everyone asking me that? I never felt better. I'm just homesick.'

'Then you should be cured soon. And your arrival in the capital will be nothing short of a Roman triumph.'

'A triumph?' The old man raised his eyebrows. 'You forget we've been defeated.'

The war correspondent sat down.

'The Nation mourns, of course,' he said sombrely. 'This campaign has indeed been a disaster.' His tone of voice changed. 'But all that is for my colleagues on the political pages to discuss. *My* concern is the human factor.' He tapped his finger on the table to stress his point. 'Your adventure is a triumph of the human spirit.'

'It'll be impossible to find much glory in our story either,' the brigadier said. 'Unless you're a writer of fiction.'

'Ah, modesty. It always hints at a great man.' The journalist took out a notebook, made a note and put it away again. 'Have you realised the parallels between your journey and that of Xenophon's Ten Thousand?'

'The *Anabasis*? We're hardly worthy of such a comparison.'

The journalist smiled.

'Who really knows what happened back then? Only

155

Xenophon. Given time and a good narrative, people will believe anything.'

'Lack of evidence also helps,' the officer said.

The journalist took out his Kodak.

'This great invention has put myths to rest,' he said.

Brigadier Nestor studied the camera.

'I like myths,' he said. 'There's more truth in them than in many facts.'

'I know what you're saying. Don't let your sadness cloud your judgement. I won't use my camera against you. A man with your experience, you ought to be able to tell a friend from a foe.'

'A man with my experience,' Brigadier Nestor echoed.

He stood and balanced himself before walking to his cot. Under his pillow was his *Lexicon of Greek and Roman Myths*. He put it on the table. The war correspondent gave it an impatient look.

'My myths are kept under lock and key,' the brigadier said and tapped the cover. 'But you, friend, want to let them loose. I hope you know what you're doing.'

The journalist shrugged.

'The story of this brigade will one day be taught in schools,' he said.

'Well, there are enough lies in the curriculum already. A few more won't make any difference.'

'Besides, in your case, my brigadier, truth isn't much of an option.'

'What do you mean?'

The war correspondent said he had interviewed several soldiers for his articles, and they had all extolled the brigadier's leadership. They believed they owed him their lives. They knew what fate many an army unit had met following the collapse of the front. Brigadier Nestor listened to the praise with suspicion.

'So?' he asked.

'But still you haven't surrendered,' the journalist said. 'Why?'

'One can't trust the enemy to treat prisoners according to the international treaties,' the officer replied. 'Surrender is not a decision to be taken lightly.'

The journalist nodded.

'Especially those prisoners responsible for the massacre of innocent civilians,' he said. 'One could understand the anger, the desire for revenge—'

'They weren't innocent,' the brigadier said before checking himself. 'I said nothing about any massacre. Whom did you talk to?'

'A journalist never reveals his sources. Basic rule of my profession.'

'That's sensitive military information,' Brigadier Nestor said. 'It's not to be disclosed. It never happened.'

'What will the punishment of the conspirators be?' the journalist asked.

The brigadier went to the crate. He picked up one of the major's books and turned to the contents page.

'A lash for every chapter of *Das Kapital*?'

The journalist did not laugh.

'Consider your reputation. They'll have to be tried here and the sentence carried out.'

'That could wait until we return home. A proper court-martial.'

'No. It's important. Consider the discipline of the troops. What'll happen if others decide to desert too?'

The senior officer shrugged.

'Let them all go to hell.'

'And we don't know how extensive the clandestine network is. What if their comrades attempt to free them?'

'What comrades?'

'There could be other Bolsheviks in the brigade, couldn't there?'

Brigadier Nestor had not thought of that.

'It'd jeopardise the rescue of your whole unit,' continued the journalist. 'You can't take any chances.'

Brigadier Nestor collapsed into a chair.

'What do you suggest?'

'Only making you immortal, brigadier. Taking those men home would only prolong their torment. The court-martial won't be any more lenient.'

This was also true. But it took away nothing from the fact that the brigadier would be staining his hands with the blood of his Chief of Staff. Brigadier Nestor shook his head. He went to the anteroom, where the orderly sat on a chair mending the holes in his superior's tunic.

'Leave that and find me four officers for trial duty,' the brigadier said.

Violetta put on a dress with a high neck and long pleated sleeves and fixed her hair with combs and pins. She inspected herself in the mirror, applied a few strokes of vermilion to her lips and left the house. She found Father Simeon in the church, sitting on the floor, polishing his glass eye with a piece of cotton daubed with alcohol.

'What do you want?' the padre asked when he saw her. 'Your visit is a desecration of this place.'

Violetta felt exhausted by her tight corset. She had not worn it in years.

'You have to help me as regards a very important and just cause,' she said.

Father Simeon blew at his glass eye and put it in.

'What mutual interest may a servant of the Lord have with a harlot?'

'Just the salvation of two lives.'

'I see. A latter-day Saint Mary of Egypt.'

'Who?'

'She lived a shameless life more than fifteen hundred years

ago until she . . . Oh, never mind.'

'I don't know her story.'

The padre was not in the mood for preaching.

'Anyway, you worry about the two traitors.'

Violetta nodded.

'I need your help.'

'Their lives are in God's hands,' the padre said.

'Not quite. They're in the hands of the brigadier.'

Father Simeon gave her a softer look.

'He wouldn't listen.'

Violetta came closer. Her heels clicked across the empty church.

'I implore you, Father.'

'It's not a matter of begging.'

'I'll come with you. The two of us—'

'I'm afraid you overestimate the powers of the flesh and the spirit. The brigadier is quite a stubborn man.'

A shaft of light from the dome lit up the woman. Father Simeon stroked his beard and said nothing for a long time. There was a solution, of course. He thought, maybe the Lord was giving him another chance by sending this woman to him.

'Father?'

'No. I'd better go alone.'

The Frenchwoman bent down to kiss his hand, but he pulled it away. She shrugged, picked up the train of her dress and started towards the door. Father Simeon's voice stopped her before she walked out.

'I haven't dictated my terms yet.'

Violetta turned and offered him a wide smile.

'*Mais bien sûr*. Anything, Father.' She walked back. 'Come by the house tonight.'

Father Simeon blushed.

'Not that,' he said. 'I'll help you only if you confess your sins and take Holy Communion.'

159

She agreed. The padre led her to the steps of the altar and asked her to kneel down.

'I'm a Catholic,' she said. 'We do things differently.'

Father Simeon hushed her with his hand.

'At least you're not an idolater. Just repeat what I say.'

It was some time since he had heard a confession. They began by reciting the Lord's Prayer, and then he asked the woman to tell him her sins. She satisfied him with a very small fraction of them.

'Is there anything else?' Father Simeon asked.

'No, Father.'

He looked into her eyes. For an instant he thought he understood why so many men wasted their lives committing carnal sin.

'Are you sure?'

'I am, Father.'

Father Simeon nodded. Next to him was his coat. He unfolded it and lifted the heavy Gospel. He began to read:

'*Peace be unto you. As my Father hath sent me, even so send I you. Whose soever sins ye remit, they are remitted unto them. And whose soever sins ye retain, they are retained.*' He motioned to her to stand. 'Now go. And I promise to do everything in my power to help.'

He was alone again. Now it was his turn to kneel before the Royal Doors and pray for the forgiveness of his own sins and for help in persuading the brigadier to show mercy.

15

'Major?'

The only light was coming from the small window in the roof. It was not enough to light the whole room. The evening was approaching fast. It was a clear sky, and the stars would soon be coming out. Major Porfirio tried to open the window. The damp winters had warped it, and it would not swing wide. He blew the cigarette smoke through the crack. In the frosty night, the smoke almost turned into crystals. Only a few days ago, he thought, the brigade had been lost in the wilderness and was tormented by the heat; now the rains threatened to drown them all, and one could not sleep without one's coat on. A few days earlier, he was also a decorated hero and the admired leader of his men . . .

'Major?'

This will be a century of change, Major Porfirio thought. He remembered the stories he had read some time ago in the news: *Industrial revolution set to reach farthest corners of Europe . . . Electrification of countryside imminent . . .* And had he not read somewhere that a regular airmail service had begun in America and some parts of Europe? He shook his head in awe. A letter sent to, let us say, Moscow that would arrive within a week – why not even a couple of days? He had been told that the flight lasted about thirty hours, but that was only because aeroplanes flew during the day. What if they could fly at night too? He attempted the calculation in his mind but did not complete it: aeroplanes reminded him of the air lieutenant.

He was surprised he did not feel hatred towards him. Rather, he was grateful. By informing on him, the aristocrat had shown the true colours of the ruling class. The incident reconfirmed the major's faith in his political beliefs. But it will not be long now, he reassured himself; the start had been made in Russia. *A spectre is haunting Europe* . . . No sooner had he repeated the first words of the *Manifesto* than his face darkened: he would not be around to witness the fulfilment of that dream. Contemplating the infinity of death, Major Porfirio shuddered a little. He did not believe, of course, in the immortality of the soul. Would he be feeling differently now if he had had a spouse? he wondered.

'Major?'

He thought, had it been a mistake not to get emotionally involved with somebody? It had not been a conscious decision. He enjoyed the occasional company of women but had never come across one who could comprehend his fascination with his profession. After a while he would invariably feel bored and lonely with any of them. At least, the Party had been the answer to his intellectual concerns. But his emotional needs had withered. Maybe if he had a child, death would not be so terrifying – a part of him to live on.

'Comrade Porfirio?'

The major turned around.

'You said something, corporal?'

In a corner of the room, beyond the reach of the moonlight, the corporal squatted with his back against the wall.

'Could you please move a little, major?'

The officer frowned.

'Move?'

'The light, major. You're blocking the light. I'm trying to read.'

Major Porfirio moved aside. The shaft of moonlight

stretched to the corner of the room. The young soldier held up a bundle of letters.

'They're from her,' he said.

Major Porfirio recognised the letters of the commissar from Salonika who had seduced the soldier into joining the Party. Lighting a cigarette, he contemplated his subordinate.

'I see.'

'I wrote her a letter,' the corporal said. 'The brigadier will see it gets delivered together with the prayer rug I picked up for her.'

The officer smoked in silence.

'He promised. Anyway, in the letter I explain what has happened. Because if she doesn't hear from me, who knows what she might think.'

'Quite.'

The moonlight fell over the pages, the hands, the young desperate face. The dim blue glow made him seem already dead.

'Killed in battle would be the obvious thing. But that's not how the mind works, is it, major?'

'I guess not.'

'More likely to assume I forgot all about her. Or that there was someone else back home all along – a wife, perhaps. It's only human to be suspicious, isn't it, comrade?'

The major smiled wryly.

'Unfortunately for us, it is.'

'She shouldn't live her life in bitterness. I think it was more than a friendship, major.' He looked at the pages with love. 'Who would've thought two people could feel so close to one another only by correspondence?'

Major Porfirio dropped his cigarette to the floor. He looked at its glowing end before pressing it with his boot. In the far corner of their prison, the corporal still talked.

'In my letter I say I risked my life to be with her because I couldn't wait. But I don't want her to think it was her fault in any way. *That's how love is,* I write. *It follows its own reasoning.'*

When the major lifted his boot, there were only a few specks of burning dust.

'The brigadier says she can have my medal. Well, it's something. I want her to be proud of me.'

He remembered that he and the major had talked about returning their decorations as a protest against the imperialist war. He asked timidly, 'Comrade, do you mind if I—?'

'Not at all, corporal. You can keep it.'

'Something to remember me by, you see.'

Major Porfirio lit another cigarette and took a long draw.

'What . . . was her name again?' he asked.

'Coralia.'

'Ah, beautiful.'

'I think so too, my major.'

From the other side of the window, the moon shone brighter than ever. The stars were out now. The major could not see the square, but it was quiet. He assumed a curfew had been imposed in advance of the execution early in the morning. He looked at the floor: the last burning bits of his cigarette had died out.

As the rubber cuff began to inflate and press his arm, Brigadier Nestor rolled his eyes.

'Do we have to do this every single time?' he asked.

The medic ignored him. He continued to squeeze the bulb until the cuff was fully inflated. Then he let the air out slowly. While listening to his stethoscope, his eyes watched the graduated rod of mercury. A moment later he deflated the cuff and removed it from his patient's arm.

'Right. Systolic one hundred and sixty, diastolic eighty-five. Hypertension.'

Brigadier Nestor rolled down his sleeve.

'Well, what do you know! I feel perfectly fine. Some

164

diseases would never have existed if the medical profession had not been invented.'

'Open your mouth, please.'

Immediately the brigadier put out his tongue. The medic was not sure whether the old man was simply obeying his instruction or meaning to be rude. He pressed the tongue with his spatula and narrowed his eyes.

'The fact of the matter is that your arteries are pumped up to bursting point. It's, of course, a reaction to your medication.'

It was his code name for the morphia. He asked the brigadier to close his mouth and returned the sphygmo-manometer to his case. He rummaged through it again and held up a rubber tube.

'You should start reducing your intake immediately, as you promised to do. Or else I shall have to push this down your oesophagus and cannulate your stomach.'

Brigadier Nestor observed the rubber tube with fear.

'Your constipation is also a side effect of your addiction,' the medic added.

The old officer curled his lip.

'The only thing I'm addicted to is the classics,' he said.

The medic did not contradict him. He put the tube back in his box and took out a large vial of morphia. Brigadier Nestor took it.

'You've been a first lieutenant for too long, medic. I'm promoting you to captain. Tell the quartermaster to sew you new shoulder boards on.'

The medic washed his hands in alcohol and shook them dry.

'My career is the last thing you should worry about. Besides, I've no intention of staying in the ranks.'

Brigadier Nestor was privy to his subordinate's aspirations.

'Oh, yes, you've told me. The founder of the Order of Discalced Physicians. Even more so then. When you're dying of hunger, the war pension will be the blessing you'd never receive from God for your charity.'

The medic tried to smile.

'Your words amount to blasphemy. Or, worse, misanthropy.'

Brigadier Nestor unlocked his trunk and hid the morphia bottle under his clothes. The medic watched him in silence. After a while he could hold back no longer.

'A summary court-martial is not perhaps the ideal way to administer justice,' he said.

That morning, in a trial which had lasted less than three hours, a tribunal of officers presided over by the brigadier had found both of the accused guilty of high treason and sentenced them to capital punishment.

Brigadier Nestor closed the lid of his trunk and locked it. 'That'll be all,' he said and hung the keys from his neck. 'Thank you.'

'Did you hear what I said? Hasn't the enemy killed enough of our men already?'

The brigadier hid the string of keys under his tunic and buttoned it up.

'If you weren't my personal physician I'd have you arrested as an agitator.'

The young doctor let out a bitter chuckle.

'An agitator? I'm just doing my job,' he said. 'Which is to save lives.'

The brigadier looked at him.

'Quite. And my job is to command this unit. So, as long as I'm in charge, *I'll* be making the decisions. Both the good and the bad ones.' He tried to smile. 'Now, it's late. If I don't go to bed soon, I'll end up in the infirmary. And neither of us wants me there.'

The young man saluted and turned to leave.

'Ah, medic,' the old man said. 'Let me have some cotton, please.'

The medic cut a piece and gave it to him. As soon as he was alone, the brigadier felt lonely. The truth was that all day he, too, had been trying to justify the court decision to himself. That it was according to the military code, was the best excuse he could think of. Feeling sad, he sat on the edge of his cot and began to remove his boots. There was a knock on the door. He gave permission to enter. It was the padre.

'You, Father. At this hour?'

Father Simeon closed the door and approached the conference table. He nodded nervously.

'Yes, yes. At this . . . the eleventh hour indeed.'

'Well?'

Father Simeon took a deep breath.

'A confession, my brigadier.'

Brigadier Nestor pulled off his boot.

'A confession?' He misunderstood. 'Listen, Father. When all this is over, I promise to sit down with you and try to remember every damn sin I ever committed.'

The padre stopped him.

'No, no, my brigadier. It's I who should be doing the talking. I know where your sword and boots are. I'm confident I can get them back. But you'll have to give me a little time.'

Brigadier Nestor put down his boot.

'If you have some idea where the stolen goods are, you only have to tell me. I'll see they're recovered. It's hardly your obligation.'

Father Simeon felt the sweat on his palms.

'Oh, but it is, my brigadier. Because *I* placed them there.'

'What are you saying, Father?'

The padre bowed his head.

'I'm the thief. Those possessions of yours and the major's . . . I stole them all.'

He had said it. He took a few steps and dropped on to a chair, his heart beating fast. He was surprised to feel relieved.

A sudden hearty laugh interrupted his thoughts of sincere remorse.

'Well done, Father. I admire your gesture. Very noble indeed. Well done. Taking the blame.'

'No, brigadier. It's nothing but the truth.'

The officer continued to laugh. Father Simeon had no option but invoke the name of God.

'I swear in the name of Lord Jesus Christ.'

Brigadier Nestor stopped laughing and looked at him. A moment later his lips formed an ambiguous smile.

'Even if it were true, Father, it'd make no difference now.'

'But why?'

'Because the men have been sentenced for high treason, not stealing.' He bent down, pulled off the second boot and threw it on the floor. 'Are you guilty of that too, Father?'

'Please, my brigadier, this isn't a joke. If you'll listen to me for a moment.'

He gave an account of his break-ins since the beginning of the withdrawal. He remembered the day and time of each theft and could name every item in the brigadier's trunk he had come across during his searches for valuables: the black uniform for evening receptions, the bundle of letters and postcards from home, the big bottle of some sort of medication – he did not know it was morphia. Sitting on the edge of his cot, barefoot, Brigadier Nestor listened. He was not entirely convinced the padre was the perpetrator of the thefts until Father Simeon mentioned the dead snake.

'I remember it perfectly,' the padre said. 'A long grey snake with a pattern of yellow diamonds.'

'Well, Father. You too will burn in Hell with the rest of us then.'

The padre blushed but did not stop. He wanted to explain his actions. He said he knew he was gambling with his soul but did it for the glory of God. His apology continued until

Brigadier Nestor began to see the sincerity of the cleric's despair. When the padre finished, the officer shrugged his shoulders.

'You'll just have to learn to live with your demons, Father. The way I have to and everyone else.'

There was not enough strength in the forgiveness to lift the padre's heart.

'You deny me my right to repent, brigadier. I regret what I've done. You have to believe me.'

Brigadier Nestor took off his braces and began to remove his breeches.

'But I do. And I pardon you.'

'I have to be punished.'

Brigadier Nestor stopped undressing and scratched his head.

'Oh, I see. Say one hundred Our Fathers.'

'You don't understand, my brigadier. You'll be doing me a favour if you arrest me.'

'Arrest you? For what? It's undoubtedly true that at the time the thefts took place I would've hanged you with pleasure. But now? Oh, I have more serious business to attend to.'

The padre's protests annoyed him. He silenced him with his hand.

'A commanding officer should know where the limits of discipline lie. Do you have any idea what the arrest of the chaplain would do to the morale of the troops? A padre stealing?'

Father Simeon bowed his head.

'I know my men aren't the most religious bunch,' the brigadier continued. 'But still, the collapse of the ultimate moral authority . . . No, it's out of the question, Father.'

'Perhaps if you spared the life of the corporal? He was only a pawn in this story.'

Brigadier Nestor shook his head.

'By killing him you condemn *me* to eternal Hell, my brigadier. I could've helped him that night.'

'You did the right thing. But if you don't think so, your present regret is sincere. Even I can see that. I'm sure God will forgive you, Father.'

'Repentance is not as easy as one assumes.'

'Listen, I'm very tired,' the brigadier said. 'You'll have to excuse me. Please go, Father. Find some other way to make amends.'

The door closed. The brigadier stared at it, shaking his head. He threw his breeches on to a chair and fell back in his cot. He thought, if there was one good soldier in that unit, it was Porfirio. He folded his hands behind his head and thought about his Chief of Staff. Then he remembered. He stood up, blocked his ears with the cotton the medic had left him and shut the windows that faced the square. Satisfied there was no way he would hear the rifles at dawn, he lay down at last in his cot and shut his eyes.

The medic hung his case behind the door, next to his smock. He stood looking at the white piece of clothing with a vacant gaze. It was torn under the arms and speckled with blood. His stethoscope hung down from a hole in its pocket, like a dead snake. On the inside of the smock, at chest height, something was written with a pen: he had copied the Hippocratic oath into all his work clothes. The more he stared at it, the more his smock turned into a map of his disappointment.

His room was the old office of the local chief of the Ottoman gendarmerie. The rest of the station housed the infirmary of the brigade. It was a single-storey building of whitewashed walls with a pitched roof and a sentry box out front. It had been abandoned soon after the Expeditionary Corps had landed on Anatolia, when the gendarmes had fled to join the army of Turkish nationalists that was already being assembled in the interior. On the wall behind the chief's

170

desk, the portrait of the Sultan once hung but now all that remained was a rectangular stain: the mayor had taken the picture down and hid it in the Town Hall to await the outcome of the war. When the situation had seemed to turn in favour of the Expeditionary Corps, he had ordered a large portrait of the King of the Greeks in a gilded frame, but it had not arrived. He was now glad it never had.

The medic turned away from the door and went across the room, trying to take his mind off the executions. The mayor had told him everything about the last occupant of that office. The chief of the gendarmerie had been an amiable man with a suntanned farmer's face, who spent a long time every morning in front of the mirror waxing his moustache. The medic sat at the desk. He rested his elbows on it, but it wobbled. He picked up one of his old medical journals from the pile on the desktop, tore off a page, folded it several times and wedged it under the table leg. He threw the journal into the rubbish bin. A moment later the weight of his action hit him. His vocation seemed to have little purpose. For the first time since he had taken up medicine, he was questioning his ability truly to better life. Many diseases had been conquered, of course. Without doubt, life expectancy had been greatly extended. But the success of medicine in prolonging life meant that a human being would now also have the chance to suffer more misery: war, famine, the death of one's children before oneself, the incapacity of old age. He rested his face in his palms that still smelt of the alcohol he had used to clean them. Once he believed it was enough to cure sickness to bring happiness. The light in the lamp on his desk flickered, and he turned the knob to let out more wick. He thought about Major Porfirio and the brigadier. *They* saw no evil in causing human suffering. Evil seemed to them as natural and indomitable a process as the rain. He did not understand their ideological differences, nor did he care to find them out now. He simplified their clash in his mind by thinking of the two men

171

as opposite ends of the same magnet. He felt tired and began to undress without getting up from his chair. No noise was coming from the other rooms. There was silence outside until the patrol that was overseeing the curfew broke it briefly as it walked down the road. Dressed in his underwear, he carried the lamp to his cot. He had only just lain down when the nurse appeared at the door. The medic gave him a blank look.

'Are you asleep, doctor?'

'Come in, nurse.'

In the near dark, his assistant removed his apron and hung it on the peg behind the door. Feeling his way, he came and sat on a chair next to the window. The moonlight lit up the side of his body like the globe a schoolteacher would use to demonstrate how night follows day. The nurse took out a handkerchief from his pocket and wiped his forehead.

'Stifling, eh?' he said.

The medic raised his head.

'What?'

'The night, doctor. Humid.'

'Uh-huh.'

The rain had passed, leaving behind large pools of evaporating water. The town was shrouded in a warm mist filled with mosquitoes. The smell of the open sewer was now worse than ever, but the troops had stayed long enough there not to notice. The nurse craned his neck and looked out the window at the moon.

'Those mosquitoes are the size of aeroplanes,' he said. 'I'm worried they'll spread malaria, doctor. There's no quinine left.'

'Don't worry. They aren't anopheles.'

The nurse rolled up his sleeve and scratched the anchor tattoo on his forearm. He began to hum. The medic covered his eyes with his arm and shifted in his cot.

'How're the sick?' he asked.

His question let loose his subordinate's eagerness to talk.

The medic listened with his arm still over his face. The nurse suddenly changed the subject.

'That corporal didn't like animals,' he said.

His superior did not react.

'They say he tried to run away because of a woman,' continued the nurse. 'He seemed like a decent enough fellow. I'm sure the brigadier considered all avenues before making his decision.'

The medic could not avoid sniggering.

'Ha. The brigadier is a—'

He wanted to say that their commanding officer was an opiate addict whose condition worsened by the day, but then he thought of the consequences of the truth if the rank and file found out: after all, the brigadier was an effigy whose supernatural authority had to be preserved if he were to sustain their hope of salvation. Besides, the revelation would contravene the principle of medical confidentiality. The medic was pleased that his present disillusionment had not, in spite of everything, erased his professional ethos completely.

'Yes, all avenues,' he said. 'I suppose you're right.'

'We owe him our lives.'

'Our lives. Indeed.'

He let his head rest on the pillow again. Against the moonlit window, the nurse nodded in appreciation. He looked at the pools of water in the street: heaps of mud rose above the surface like islands seen from afar. The spectacle reminded him of home.

'I hope I'll see it again,' he said.

The medic turned his head.

'What was that?'

'My home, doctor. It's been over a year since my last leave.'

His superior sighed.

'Oh, it'll still be there.'

'There's a small hospital in the capital,' the nurse said. 'But not enough staff.'

173

'I see.'

'There's one doctor who's too old to operate any more, a few nurses and an intern who never got his degree. They can use all the help they can get. When I go back, I'll join them.'

'That's good.'

It was very late. The nurse stopped talking and contemplated the moon. The medic covered himself with the blanket and tried to imagine the sound of the sea.

Part 3

The Sea

16

In the afternoon the sun came out and baked the mud left behind the receding floodwaters. When the clay began to dry, something strange happened: the earthen streets of the town, the yards, the park and the gardens all turned red. First to witness the miracle was Yusuf. The Arab was in the main square, sweeping with a broom the spot where the two soldiers had fallen, when the dust under his slippers began to change colour. Thinking that the blood of the executed was staining the town, he shook with fear.

'*A'uwudhu billah iminash Shaitan ir rajeem*,'* he prayed.

He was not the only one to believe that evil was visiting the small town. Soon the rest of the townspeople rose from their afternoon nap in their underwear, their gowns and nightcaps and saw the change from their windows. They climbed down the stairs, opened their doors, came out into the street, dazed, and watched in silence. The bravest scratched the earth to convince themselves it was not an illusion of the sun: the red mud stained their hands.

At that time the schoolmaster was in the grocery. The draught from the open door carried in the voices. He put down the brandy bottle.

'Whom are they going to shoot now?' he wondered.

The grocer slept with folded arms and his head against the counter. Mr Othon decided not to wake him up. That day at

---

*'I seek refuge in Allah from Satan the rejected' (Arabic).

the execution the schoolmaster had tried again to speak to Violetta, but she had rebuffed him. He had found refuge in the grocery, where he had been drinking all morning. He staggered to the door. Outside, soldiers were joining the townspeople, and the unrest was growing. The schoolmaster gave them a scornful look.

'I loved her,' he hiccuped. 'I admit it. Now, leave me alone.'

No one paid him any attention. The earth reflected the sunlight, turning the walls of the houses red too. When the wind began to blow, a cloud of red dust rose in the air and swallowed up the people. Everyone, apart from the schoolmaster, rushed to find shelter.

'She's the Devil,' he stammered from the veranda of the grocery. 'Never ever trust a woman, friends. Especially one from France.'

He held the brandy bottle and took a swig from it. The wind blasted his face with dust, but he did not seem to care. The dust entered the shops and the houses through the doors and the windows and settled on the furniture and the carpets. At last he began to understand what was happening but still looked around him serenely. Behind him the grocer had woken up and was running to the windows to shut them.

'This is Hell,' the Armenian said.

'This is nothing,' Mr Othon said. 'Not being loved, that's Hell, my friend.'

He raised the bottle, but it was empty. He threw it away and stepped forward, but where he thought the step was, his foot found no support. Falling from the height of the veranda, he landed face down on the dry red mud.

Lying in bed Violetta listened to her maid dashing to defend the house from the whirlwind. She turned her head towards the window. 'Where's that priest to tell us about the ten plagues,' she said and adjusted the compress on her forehead.

She spent no more time thinking about the incident; her mind was occupied with the execution.

The padre had failed to save the two lives. On her way home from the square, the town had seemed to her smaller, as if the houses had sunk several inches under the weight of the crime. She had not expected the event to affect her so much. She wished now she had not witnessed it. Somewhere in the house, a heavy shutter banged against the window. She heard her maid climb the stairs, enter a room and latch the shutter.

Later the wind eased off, and the red dust began to fall quietly over the town. Violetta considered her plan for a long time. Having made up her mind, she reached for the bell on the night table. Annina answered her call in a state of panic.

'What a disaster, Madame!' she said. 'The curse of the dead is falling on our heads, no?'

'Calm down, my sweet. That dust is a curse only to my wardrobe. Have you sealed all the windows?'

Her maid assured her that she had taken care of everything. She had blocked the gaps with wet towels and also the chimney of the fireplace.

'But the rose bushes are at the mercy of the dust, Madame.'

Her mistress shrugged.

'Never mind. I always thought that garden was too beautiful for this forsaken place.'

The dust continued to fall outside, settling on the roofs, the trees, the pavements. Looking out, Violetta began to understand how such a spectacle could be mortifying to the ingenuous. She remembered a visit to Pompeii many years earlier: the walls, the collapsed colonnades, the baths, the shops and houses. Scattered among the ruins had been the remains of hundreds of victims preserved by the rain of ash and cinder; men, women and children, aristocrats, freemen and slaves, gladiators in chains, animals. The memory made her flesh crawl. Annina was still standing at the door.

179

'Start packing, *jolie*,' she said. 'It's time we left this place.'

Annina opened her mouth, but her mistress interrupted her:

'But first go and tell the mayor I want to see him.'

The maid left, closing the door softly. Violetta got out of bed and put on her robe. In one of her closets, she found an empty box and set about carrying out her decision. First she picked up her kimono, folded it with affection and placed it in the bottom of the box. In the back of her wardrobe, she found the fur coat made from eleven foxes and the wide hat with the bunch of pearls arranged like grapes. The embroidered umbrella with the silver handle was hanging from the rail. She emptied her jewellery box on her bed and found the garter with the amethysts.

The box was almost filled when her maid informed her that the mayor had arrived. Violetta asked her to show him into the drawing room. When she went to meet him, he was wiping his face with his handkerchief.

'Terrible, terrible,' he said. 'That dust. It's infernal. Can you believe that some simpletons are talking of abandoning the town?'

'The execution has probably shocked them more than the red dust,' Violetta said.

The mayor put his handkerchief back in his pocket.

'Of course. A regrettable event. I'm sorry my people had to witness it. All these years of the war I tried to keep us safe. And I succeeded, didn't I? In any case, those two were enemies of the State. Why should we care?'

'An execution is a terrible event. Two are even worse.'

The mayor nodded.

'But the army is now leaving and things can go back to normal,' he said. 'The war is over.'

The Frenchwoman watched the dust falling outside her window.

'*Plus ça change*,' she said.

'Exactly,' the mayor said. 'Everything is going to be fine.'

'That's not what I said.'

The mayor noticed she was wearing her robe. He wondered what had happened to the kimono he had given her.

'No? You should start speaking the language of your future husband. You've lived in this place long enough to have learned it.'

'My education was always the least of your concerns. Kama Sutra. Ha!'

The mayor bit his lip.

'Othon was right. You *are* a suffragist.'

She removed her ring and put it in with his other gifts. Only then did the mayor see the box.

'These belong to you,' she said. 'You should send some people for the bath. It's too heavy for me and Annina to carry downstairs.'

The mayor frowned.

'The bath? But . . . what about us?'

Ever since the beginning of their affair he had tried several times to teach himself his lover's language, but he was too impatient to learn. That afternoon, for the first time, he had no trouble understanding her words perfectly when she spoke up again:

'*Nous? Notre histoire est finie.*'

Air Lieutenant Kimon made his way through the crowd and fled from the square with his hand over his mouth. As soon as he turned the corner, he vomited against the wall. While leaning over he heard the pistol deliver the *coups de grâce*. He had helped to send the major to his death. His intent had only been to humiliate him. He had found him excessively self-important and self-righteous, that was all. He spat again. He did not think a man deserved to die because of his beliefs. The Chief of Staff's socialist convictions did not bother him;

it was authority he had a grudge against. He wiped his mouth with the back of his hand. A voice intruded on his grief.

'A historic occasion, don't you think? One feels humbled to have witnessed it.'

It was the war correspondent.

'What?' the airman asked.

'The last dead of the war.' The journalist raised his hands in the air. 'God willing, of course.'

His camera hung round his neck. He noticed that the airman was looking at it.

'It's all captured here for future generations,' he said.

'Perhaps future generations would rather forget all this.'

'I don't agree, lieutenant. Historians, students, the descendants of this heroic brigade. They'll all need to understand what happened.'

'And you shall endeavour to explain.'

The journalist nodded.

'Both the glory and the suffering.'

For a while neither man spoke. But the journalist could not hold back his excitement.

'Conspiracy, a desperate act of love, an elusive and unpatriotic thief, a great leader. It'll be the best story written about this war.'

'The story of two men shot.'

'Yes, what a culmination. As in a Greek tragedy, eh?'

In the town square, the silent crowd started to disperse. Air Lieutenant Kimon contemplated the naked tamarisks, the wall of sandbags against which the two men had stood, the firing squad now walking away in step.

'Glory,' he scoffed. 'There was little glory back there. I hope you took enough photographs.'

The correspondent shrugged.

'Bad things happen whether one is there to photograph them or not, lieutenant.'

The airman remembered the dispatches he had read without much thought throughout the war: the elegant descriptions of battle, the formality of the text, the explicit photographic plates that caused no grief.

Behind him the journalist was still talking: '. . . It was a practice of barbaric nations to execute the bearers of displeasing news.'

The mayor wandered down the streets, lost in his thoughts. He felt humiliated and terrified. His rejection by his fiancée had been unexpected. He looked in the box he carried in his arms and felt the expensive fabrics. How could she do this to him? The red dust fell over him and settled on the expensive gifts in the box: the diamond tiaras, the velvet slippers, the *Compagnie des Indes* porcelain figurines. He looked around but did not recognise his town. The once-whitewashed walls, the pavements, the trees and gardens had all turned red. He shuddered. A few people still stood under the eaves of the shops and watched. The mayor hitched up the box and took the road to the Town Hall. Not long after, he saw a man lying in the middle of the road and covered in dust.

'Othon?'

When he received no reply, he put the box down and knelt beside his former friend. Holding his breath he placed his palm on the schoolmaster's back. He was relieved to find he was alive.

'Can you hear me?'

The schoolmaster did not move. The mayor turned him gently over and cleaned his face. The dust still fell. Behind it the afternoon sun baked the earth. Slowly the schoolmaster opened an eye a little then shut it again.

'Take your dirty hands off me,' he said.

The mayor felt a sense of relief.

'Thank God. For a moment I—'

He held the man's head in his arms: it felt heavy and

lifeless. The schoolmaster was unshaven, his hair was dirty, his breathing seemed to be coming from very far away.

'Go away,' Mr Othon said. 'Leave me alone.'

'What happened?' Then the mayor smelt the alcohol. 'If this is over Madame Violetta, I can tell you—'

The schoolmaster's lips formed a mocking smile.

'Violetta? Who cares. I was just testing a new fermentation method for the Chemistry class.'

He shook off the other man's hands, rested on his elbows and squinted around him with disapproval: the shut doors and shutters, the people under the verandas watching the dust come down.

'I hope I live long enough to watch her go to Hell,' he said. 'And you too. Holding her hand all the way. After that I could die in peace.' He scratched the ground with his nails and scooped up a handful of red dust. He studied it closely. 'Haematite,' he said. 'Washed down from the hills. That explains it.'

He threw away the dust and wiped his hand on his trousers. He was recovering his senses. The bottle he had been drinking from lay beyond his reach.

'Pass me that bottle,' he ordered.

The mayor gave it to him, but it was empty.

'That figures,' Mr Othon said. 'He stole my woman, he steals my brandy too.'

The rain of dust was petering out. The air began to clear but was still hot.

'There's something you should know,' the mayor said.

He sat on the ground and broke the news of his rejection to his friend. His account was quiet and melancholy. What eased his pain was knowing that the story would have a healing influence on his friend. He was right. The schoolmaster's spirits seemed to rise.

'You were always a fool for love, mayor,' Mr Othon said. 'Take my word for it, she's not worth it.'

184

The mayor gave him an injured look.

'Perhaps she was too good for this place. An angel who fell to Earth.'

'An angel? Ha. Yes, I loved her once too, but what could you expect from a man condemned to abstinence? Her bed was the garden of earthly delights. Fine. But marriage? You've been lucky to get out in time, believe me. Can you imagine the ridicule that'd follow you, a state official, everywhere in Anatolia?'

'Things are changing, Othon,' the mayor said. 'I've the feeling I won't be an official for long. When the dust of this war settles, there'll be elections. A man of Christian descent will never be allowed to retain his post. Especially after the passing of this army.'

Mr Othon grinned.

'The unsoundness of your fiscal decisions over the years might also have something to do with it.'

The mayor gave the box with Violetta's gifts a sorrowful look.

'I regret nothing. It's a pity though that all I have to remind me of her is a box of clothes and an iron bath.'

A morbid sensation came over him. He brushed off the dust on his jacket. The dust storm had stopped, and the towns-people were coming out of their shelter.

'I tried not to take sides in this war. I wanted our town to be neutral. Everything was fine until those devils came marching in.'

He raised his head and turned it left and right. All he saw was misfortune: the cracked clay earth, the shopfronts buried in dust, the square where the executions had taken place.

'Armageddon,' he said. 'Many are preparing to go. The defeat had sowed the fear of reprisals against Christians. This morning's executions made things worse. And then came the dust.'

The schoolmaster threw away the empty brandy bottle.

185

'I'm not staying here much longer either.'

'You're leaving too?'

The schoolmaster removed his shoe and emptied the dust out of it.

'I've decided to follow the army back to the land of our forefathers.'

'What land? You were born here.'

'There's nothing left for me here to call home.'

The mayor bit his moustache. The news increased his gloom. He became aware of muffled talk around him and pricked up his ears: the townspeople were discussing their plans for departure. The schoolmaster continued.

'Like you said, it's safe to stay. There've been executions and evictions elsewhere already. Our number could come up soon.' He raised his hands. 'It's understandable.'

'We harmed nobody.'

Mr Othon shrugged.

'We harboured the invaders, didn't we?'

The smell of the open sewer blew in their direction and sank the mayor's hopes too.

'Perhaps the people are right,' he said. 'Hell has come to the surface. Look at the dust.'

Once they had interpreted the dust storm as a supernatural sign, the townspeople began to discover mystical meaning in all the events that had taken place in their town recently: the arrival of the brigade, the rising of sewage in the open conduit, the flood, the executions: they were warnings they had to leave before anything worse happened.

'Don't tell me you believe that nonsense, too?' the schoolmaster asked the mayor.

He tried to persuade him that there was nothing super-natural about the random phenomena, but the mayor's shame at the embezzlement of the town funds, his sadness for the loss of his love, his fear of the future had given way to a sudden determination. He brushed his trousers, buttoned up his jacket and straightened his tie. The confusion of his life had put itself instantly in order. 'My fellow citizens,' he said, raising his voice. 'I'm here to help you.' They all listened in silence. He had given his speech and received many warm handshakes when he called to mind the schoolmaster's question.

'It doesn't matter what *I* believe, Othon. I have to bow to the democratic view of the majority. Therefore it's my obligation to lead these people to safety. Damn it, am I not the head of this municipality?'

'And those poor souls are so terrified they'll follow you like Moses.'

The mayor smiled.

'They'd better. I know the safest route to the coast.'

He turned and kicked the box at his feet. It went rolling across the street, scattering on the red dust ornaments, fabrics and shoes.

'Yes, I can guide them and the army to the sea,' he said. 'I'll only need a little help.'

'From me?' the schoolmaster asked.

'Not from you, Othon. From the Scouts.'

17

The gearbox that drove the magneto of the radiotelegraph had been crushed by a piece of the roof of the headquarters, during the enemy bombardment on the first day of the counter-attack, back in August. The situation had been critical: communications with the defending battalions along the front had to be restored quickly. The orderly had found a bicycle in the farmhouse where the brigade command had been established and adapted it so that it turned the magneto.

He checked the time, sat on the seat and slowly began to pedal. Through the door to the conference room came the sound of snoring: the brigadier was still asleep. The rear wheel of the bicycle gathered speed. A belt made of trouser braces set the magneto in motion. The orderly looked outside. In the square the Arab was sweeping the dust where the two conspirators had fallen earlier that morning.

The sun came out. From his seat on the bicycle, the orderly witnessed the spectacle of the town turning red. It haunted him no less than it did the townspeople. He crossed himself but did not stop. When the magneto was turning fast, he jumped off the bicycle. He sat at the radiotelegraph and put on the headphones. He keyed a brief message then held his breath and listened, turning the dial a little from time to time, while the magneto slowed down. When the magneto stopped, he removed the headphones with disappointment but no surprise.

In the square civilians and soldiers came out of houses and shops and inspected the red earth. From this distance the orderly could not hear what they were telling each other. He sat on the bicycle and started to pedal again. While the heavy machine gathered speed, a windstorm broke out, and the crowd outside scattered. The young man watched the wind shrouding everything in dust. The pedals turned under his boots, and the rusty chain rotated the rear wheel noisily. He felt he was carrying out a ritual that had as little purpose and meaning as the daily raising of the flag. He stopped to shut the window and started to pedal again, feeling the sweat on his back and under his arms. From behind the door, the sound of snoring ceased. The orderly sat at the radiotelegraph again.

He was about to give up when he heard something through the interference. He turned the dial carefully. It was not until the wind outside had dropped that he was able to hear it clearly. On a piece of paper, he jotted down a series of dots and dashes. Following a few brief exchanges, he threw away the headphones and walked into the conference room without knocking. The brigadier was on his cot. Holding up the piece of paper with the deciphered Morse broadcast, the orderly opened his mouth but saw that under the blanket Brigadier Nestor did not stir. The boy shivered.

'My brigadier?'

His commanding officer gave no indication of hearing. The soldier stretched out his arm and shook him. The old officer jumped. He sat up and removed the cotton he had plugged his ears with before going to bed.

'What's the meaning of this, orderly? Did I tell you to wake me up?

'My brigadier, thank God. I thought you were—'

'Dead?'

The old man turned to the window: it was over. The view of the empty square filled him with remorse.

'I'm afraid not. Then at least I'd have an hour's sleep in peace. What is it?'

'The radio, sir,' the boy said excitedly. 'We've made contact.'

He said that he had exchanged messages with the remnants of the Expeditionary Corps that had fled to the islands. Brigadier Nestor started to laugh.

'The gods just play with us,' he said.

He jumped out of bed with a liveliness he had not shown for a long time and issued his order: they were leaving the town.

The preparations went on through the night. At dawn the brigade was ready to march. The dromedaries were arranged in a long train, and the reins of each animal were tied to the tail of the one before. The mules were fed and watered, the tanks of the lorries were filled, and the stretchers with the wounded were loaded on to them. Very little equipment was to be carried on that final stretch of the journey. Most of it was left behind, including the artillery guns that had made it so far: they were no longer needed. Their breechblocks were removed, their carriages were broken to pieces and the last unfired shells were thrown off the edge of a deep ravine at the outskirts of the town. When the brigadier came out of the Town Hall that morning, the town resembled a scrapyard. In addition to the field guns, scattered everywhere were spare engine parts, wooden cartwheels, empty petrol cans, tents and camp beds. Brigadier Nestor surveyed the landscape of defeat: on the roof of the Town Hall, the flag of the brigade flapped like a vulture. Despite his previous night's sleep, a feeling of exhaustion sat on his shoulders. The sound of his lorry with his orderly behind the wheel took Brigadier Nestor away from his thoughts.

The troops were lining up in the square. The wall of sandbags against which the two men had stood had been unmade overnight. The bloodied dust had been cleaned. In the courtyard of the Town Hall, in the small garden with the marble bust, were two unmarked crosses over a patch of churned earth. Brigadier Nestor observed his army with feverish eyes. That morning he had taken a large dose of morphia, but it had yet to take effect.

190

The soldiers had found their companies, and the horsemen had taken their positions when the crowd of civilians entered the square, led by the troop of Scouts. Despite having been informed of the townspeople's decision to follow the brigade, the brigadier was still taken by surprise. Every man, woman and child seemed to carry as much weight as their pack animals. Heavily laden with the rest of their belongings, their oxcarts turned furrows in the street. There were tables and chairs, wall clocks and framed portraits, birdcages, cooking pans, wardrobes, mattresses. Lost in the crowd were sheep, chickens and cows that made a great noise. Brigadier Nestor knitted his brows; the desperate exodus reminded him of a carnival parade. Dressed in his Scoutmaster's uniform, the mayor signalled to the crowd to halt. He came forward and saluted cheerfully. His Victrola was loaded on to a donkey.

'At your command, my brigadier.'

The officer clasped his hands behind his back. From the steps of the Town Hall, he gave the crowd a scornful look and tapped his foot.

'We aren't going to the bazaar, mayor.'

The mayor turned and looked at his people with uncertainty. Seeing nothing strange, he shrugged his shoulders.

'It's not just items of sentimental value,' he said. 'How else would we pay for food and lodging where we're going?'

'Don't worry about that. I'm sure the motherland will provide for you all,' the brigadier replied.

There was nothing the mayor could do. Quietly he unloaded his Victrola from the donkey and placed it on the steps of the Town Hall. Then he ordered the townspeople to do the same with their own belongings. It did not end there. The brigadier gave the order to slaughter all animals that were not coming along and instructed his men to place the civilians in the middle of the column. The mayor and his Scouts joined the vanguard because they would be leading them to the sea.

*

Brigadier Nestor had climbed into his lorry when Father Simeon came to see him. The brigadier had not seen the padre since the night before the executions when he had come to beg clemency for the two men. That night Father Simeon had visited the condemned to pray with them and offer them the sacrament. The major had declined, but the corporal had partaken of Communion. It was some sort of consolation to the padre, who was still tortured by remorse for the night at the steps of Saint Gregorius Theologus when he had refused him admission. But his relief had been temporary. The following dawn, as he administered the last rites over the bodies of the two soldiers, his depression had returned, and had been heavier than before.

'My brigadier,' he said. 'A word, if you please?'

Brigadier Nestor looked at his watch.

'Please make it brief.'

Father Simeon climbed on to the back of the lorry. It was a while since he had been inside, but everything seemed to be in the same place: the heavy trunk, the stove, the table laid with maps, the holster hanging from the crossbar of the tarpaulin. Brigadier Nestor sat on the edge of his cot. There was still a layer of dust on the items that had not been carried to the Town Hall when the brigadier had taken up residence there. It prompted the padre to recall their earlier journey through the wilderness almost with fondness. That was the time when the enemy was the Devil; when evil was what they escaped from and good was where they were headed. The padre longed for the simplicity their lives had attained during their adventure. The suffering, the shortage of food, the desolation: it all truly purified the soul, as any hermit would know. He wondered, why did it matter whether the troops came to his church or not? Gradually, unbeknown to himself, each man was turning into a little saint. If only they had never come across the town but had gone wandering through the wilderness for ever . . . Because the death of the flesh was trivial compared to the exaltation of the soul, Father Simeon thought. When he spoke up, his voice trembled a little.

'My brigadier, I ask permission to stay behind.'

The officer puffed. He removed his cap and scratched his head.

'What's the problem this time, Father?'

The padre looked around him for somewhere to sit. There was nowhere; the back of the lorry was full of clutter. Standing he felt like an accused man in the dock. As soon as he opened his mouth, the words came. He talked about his lifelong dream of becoming a missionary, his loss of courage to fulfil his ambition as a young priest and the doldrums of his insignificant parish later.

'There has to be more a cleric could do,' he said. 'Don't you think so, brigadier?'

The officer did not answer.

'Yes,' the padre continued. 'There has to be. I volunteered for the campaign three years ago, having had no idea what I was looking for, but I found it at last.'

'You have?' Brigadier Nestor asked.

'My calling is to stay in this town that has no priest and be the shepherd of its people.'

'Haven't you noticed the crowd outside, Father? In a moment there won't be a single Christian left here.'

'The destitute of the slum, my brigadier. And the Muslims. *They* are my flock. I intend to establish a holy mission and convert them to the true faith.'

Brigadier Nestor felt pity for him.

'Don't worry about them, Father. They're the victors in this war.'

'But they worship a lie, brigadier. What about their souls?'

Brigadier Nestor searched for his cigars. Then he remembered that the padre had, of course, stolen them some time before.

'Let them believe a lie. It's easier.'

'You talk like a casuist.'

The old officer puffed.

'Are you sure of your decision, Father?'

The padre nodded.

'I believe it's my destiny, my duty and my penance.'

'I see. Well, your spiritual guidance will be missed.'

Father Simeon smiled bitterly.

'I wish that were true.'

The brigadier looked the cleric in the eye. For an instant he thought he detected the beginnings of insanity.

'Very well. You may stay. The army is grateful for your services.'

He opened his trunk. From the tunic of his parade uniform, he unpinned a medal and held it out to the padre.

'I can't remember what this was for, but it couldn't have been for anything braver than your decision, Father.'

Father Simeon raised his hands in refusal.

'No, no, my brigadier, I can't accept it. If there is any reward to be had, I shall receive it from other quarters.'

The old officer shrugged and threw the medal back in the trunk. When he offered his hand, the padre shook it warmly. He jumped off the lorry, and the dog came up to him, wagging its tail. Father Simeon smiled and patted it on the head.

'Of course you can stay, Caleb,' he said. 'You can be my deacon.'

Padre and dog watched the lowering of the flag from the roof of the Town Hall. A bugle sounded the order to march. Like the heavy carriages of a train pulling out of a station, one after another the column of troops and civilians slowly started to move.

Yusuf walked behind the dromedaries, carrying a suitcase in either hand. He was panting. The pack animals travelled quietly, leaving behind a trail of dung.

'Just as I thought,' he said. 'The smell of the town is coming along, too.'

Beside him Annina walked with the mayor's cat in her arms. The maid was sweating too. Her long skirt of black brocade trailed behind her, grazing the dirt and was caught in the briers. The next time she stopped to free her dress, Yusuf puffed with impatience.

'That dress is too long. One ought to wear trousers in the mountain.'

His lover lifted her skirt and stepped over the briers.

'I'm fine. The day women start wearing trousers, they'll also start to fight in your wars.'

There was little talk among the others. The noise was mostly from the lorry engines up ahead and the animals. The vultures had long noticed the winding line that made its way across the hills and followed it quietly from high above. Some time later a whistle was heard, and the muleteers halted their animals. Yusuf put down the suitcases and sat on them. Annina joined him, and he began to stroke the cat in her lap.

'We're going to the sea, cat. There're more fish there than even you could eat.'

The cat closed her eyes and purred, digging her claws into the thick brocade. Suddenly the birds flew off the trees and scattered in the sky. The vultures arrived, sat on the branches and folded their wings, standing like emblems of ancient kingdoms. Annina pulled a handkerchief from her cuff and wiped the sweat off her lover's brow.

'*Mon petit* Yusuf. You're the bravest man I've ever known.'

The Arab grinned with mock pride.

'The bravest gardener in Anatolia,' he said.

Not far away Violetta, dressed in a chiffon jacket and holding her parasol, stood and watched the horizon. The coast was still out of sight. The whistle sounded, and they had to rejoin the caravan. Soon the column was moving again. It was a narrow trail, and several times the mules, dazed by the sun, tottered and came close to the edge before the drivers brought them back. Their braying woke up Brigadier Nestor from his nap. He sat up in his cot and rubbed his eyes with his fists. He moved aside a flap of the torn canvas and looked out. Leading the column was the troop of Scouts.

He turned to look at the dim interior of his lorry. Everything was there: his trunk, the stove, the table with his maps, his holster hanging from the roof. For a moment he toyed with the idea that he had never ordered the massacre, that the brigade had not marched into the town, that his Chief of Staff was still alive. The coffee smoked in the pot. He filled his cup and drank, thinking about the major.

He tried to remember, did he have a shot of morphia that morning? He could hardly believe that he had: he felt tired. He decided to have one now. The syringe was in its usual place, but he could not find the rubber band. He removed his belt instead to tie round his arm, but first he had to boil the syringe. The stove was cooling down; he had to build the fire up. He took the scoop and dug it in the bucket with the coal but came up only with ash.

'Orderly!'

The driver's hatch opened.

'I need coal for the stove.'

The lorry slowed down.

'I'm afraid there isn't any, my brigadier,' the orderly said, keeping his eyes on the track.

'Don't tell me it was *stolen*?'

'No, my brigadier. We ran out.'

Brigadier Nestor raised his hands in resignation. Even a simple gesture was difficult to carry out: his arms felt heavy. A voice inside him told him to hold on; it would not be long now, the coast was near. He had saved his men. He thought of the padre and his decision to stay behind. He wished he, too, had gone insane. Perhaps the next shot of morphia would be the one to tip the scale. He was prepared to use the syringe without boiling it when he noticed the box with Major Porfirio's books. He called to his orderly.

'What is this doing here?'

The soldier had a quick look back.

'The evidence from the court-martial, my brigadier. I thought you wished to keep it.'

Brigadier Nestor lifted the hot plate with the pair of tongs and dropped one of the books into the stove. While he waited for it to catch fire, he picked up a few volumes and turned the pages. He threw another book in the fire before returning the rest to the box.

'Maybe I could ask the cook, my brigadier. There's coal in the field kitchen. If we stop for a moment?'

'No. No more stops until we reach the coast.'

Brigadier Nestor shut the hatch and placed the syringe in the pot. Waiting for the water to boil, he rolled up his sleeve and tied his belt above his elbow. He injected the morphia and left the syringe on his desk. His eyelids flapped a few times and then shut. He thought he heard noise outside and half opened his eyes. He could see nothing. He stretched out his hand, feeling along the tarpaulin for the flap. As soon as he moved the cover aside, the sunlight burned his eyes: the lorry had reached the top of a hill. Ahead of them was the sea. He squinted at the sun. On the shore he saw the standing doorposts of ancient mausoleums, amid pieces of fallen columns, tombstones slipping slowly into the sea and sarcophagi ravaged by the centuries, half sunk in the sand and the waves. In the gulf beyond the coastal necropolis, he made out a small fleet. And far beyond them, he thought he saw the faint shapes of the islands of the homeland.

His joy lasted for only a moment. Soon he began to suspect that the ruins, the sea, the ships and the islands were all a deception of the morphia. He let the flap drop, and in the darkness of the lorry he felt desperately under the covers not for the vial with the drug or his letters from home but for his *Lexicon of Greek and Roman Myths*. When he found it, he held it in his arms, fell back on his cot and shut his eyes.

It was several hours after the departure of the column of soldiers and civilians, a long time since the dust raised by feet, hoofs and wheels had settled and the neighing of the pack animals had faded, after the smell of exhausts had cleared and the stench of the open sewer had returned that the people of the slum found the courage to come out of their homes. They crossed the moat around their neighbourhood, tiptoed towards the silent market and pressed their faces to the glass to see inside the shut windows. The bravest chanced as far as the square, where they were confronted by a terrible sight: scattered across the open space were the carcasses of slaughtered animals, pieces of expensive furniture, bundles of clothes and rolled-up carpets. For a while they did not dare to touch them, in case someone would accuse them of stealing, until they realised there was no one around. In the courtyard of the Town Hall, they came upon two crosses over a patch of turned earth and puzzled over them for a while, trying to understand why these dead had not been buried in the cemetery. Only when they noticed that there was no flag on the mast of the Town Hall did they convince themselves that they were alone in the town and climb the marble steps that led to the double doors. They felt the chill of the official tiles on the bare soles of their feet, heard the echo of their whispers with suspicion and began to search the rooms for valuables. There was a lot, but little of it they could carry: neither the mahogany floors nor the cast-iron railings of the gallery would have been easy to pull out, and they would have had to break the marble conference table into several pieces to get it out the door. In the library they threw to the floor the rare manuscripts and papyri and climbed on them to search behind the cobwebs for secret compartments, but there were not any. They were pulling apart an invaluable Gutenberg bible in case it hid a key to a medieval trapdoor somewhere in the municipal building – a book that centuries earlier a monk had brought from the library of the Patriarchate some time after the sacking of Constantinople – when the unexpected tolling of bells sent a chill down their spines.

They followed the sound to the Christian church and gaped up at the belfry, where the enormous bells swayed, and for a moment they were convinced they were looking at the ghost of a Christian saint until the tolling stopped, the door of the church opened, and they recognised the priest. He walked out with his arms spread wide and a strange smile on his face, followed by the dog. No matter how much he tempted them with salvation, begged them with tears in his eyes or threatened them with eternal hellfire while calling himself the Apostle of All Anatolians, he only managed to frighten the children with his words. They decided that the poor man had lost his reason, and there was nothing they could do for him.

The crowd resumed its search. By the time they reached the Frenchwoman's house, they had worked themselves into a frenzy. The greedy burst into the bedrooms and attacked the armoured safes with crowbars, the contemptuous came up with profane acts to honour the regime of her lover the mayor that had sentenced them to poverty and sickness, the angry began to burn, tear or break anything they could salvage from the hands of the looters, the sensible headed for the kitchen, the pantry and the cellar searching for food. It was midnight when they finished, and they lay under the stars to put the children to sleep. At dawn they found the few buffalo that had survived the bayonets of the soldiers, yoked them to their carts, which they had loaded with the abandoned treasures, and, seeing that the tracks of the army led west to the coast, they themselves left the town in the opposite direction, where a fine October sun rose slowly above the Anatolian hills.

www.vintage-books.co.uk